"A charming and very romantic story with lots of laughs along the way. The ending puts a perfect cap on the story. I look forward to reading more books in this series to see what happens to some of my favorite supporting characters."

—Fresh Fiction

"Ah, l'amour. I adored this story and the wonderful hero and heroine, who shed all their inhibitions and fears in order to go on the most powerful journey they ever embarked on ... falling in love."

—Smexy Books

"An exciting and sweet historical love story. It has everything that I look for in a good fairy-tale retelling while also tying back to Bradley's earlier books. I am really excited to see more of this series, particularly because of the out-of-control but still entertaining Worthington family."

—Feminist Fairy Tale Reviews

"A laugh-out-loud-funny novel from Celeste Bradley, the third in the Wicked Worthingtons series. Lighthearted but with a few profound moments, it is filled with deception, misunderstanding, exaggeration, cross-dressing, and mistaken identity."

—Harlequin Junkie

While You Were Dreaming

The Haven Holiday Series

New York Times Bestselling Author

CELESTE BRADLEY

This book is for Dottie.
Your kindness is a beautiful influence in the world.

Acknowledgments

I must acknowledge several people for their hard work in bringing *While You Were Dreaming* to life.

First of all, the writers of the film *While You Were Sleeping*, Daniel G. Sullivan and Fredric Lebow. We all owe them gratitude for giving us a new classic holiday film, one that inspired me to write *While You Were Dreaming* as a tribute to such a marvelous story.

I must also thank my wonderful team here at CelesteBradley.com. Charlie Fitch, Darbi Gill, and Geneva Craven Schult, your generosity and brilliance are so necessary to everything that I do.

Prologue

I N THE SNOWY north of England, in a valley in Staffordshire, there lies a pretty little community known as Haven. It is perhaps the ideal English village. As one follows a curving road along the ice-covered River Churnet, one comes upon prosperous little farms, blanketed in white. These give way to tidy stone cottages with warmly glowing windows, that open out upon a welcoming village square lined with shops and vital local businesses that, during the weeks leading up to Christmas Day, not even the deterrent of winter's chill can empty.

There is a talented blacksmith with a busy smithy, a welcoming innkeeper with a comfortable establishment, a practical but creative milliner who can give the most common straw bonnet that special Sunday touch, and a very fine church built of local stone with proper stained glass windows and a spacious vicarage beyond it.

The village is well supported by the needs of the fine manor that lies just over the river, and of course the people of Haven help each other in times of need—but there is something else afoot in this enchanting little place that has nothing to do with his lordship's gold.

Haven is where one comes to find the single thing coin cannot buy.

Chapter 1

VICAR JOHN BARTON took the last nail into his hand and hefted his hammer once more. Pounding the finishing nail into the last framing board around the final window of the entire house should have been a triumph. The large but drafty old vicarage had been reborn into a spacious, snug home bright with fresh paper on the walls and fine glass windows. He'd begun the work when he'd first arrived in Haven a little over two years past. Only the painting of the last few window frames remained.

John should have been exultant. Instead he only felt edgy and cold.

It was not the proper season for building. It was December, lacking only a few days until Christmas. And December in Staffordshire was no summer day in Brighton!

Yet John had been determined to finish his vicarage. Furthermore, he needed to keep busy so as not to dwell upon the lord of Havensbeck and his lady, getting ready to put on their first Christmas celebration as a wedded couple at the manor. All of Haven was invited. John's invitation had been penned by her ladyship herself, the warm greeting simple, the wistful request an act of reconciliation toward a family friend.

He would never receive any other sort of message from her now. That ship had sailed, that stable door had been left open, that water had turned to ice under the bridge—and Matthias was a bloody, greedy poaching bastard!

Except he wasn't. Lord Matthias was a good man and a dedicated, responsible landlord who took excellent care of Haven and all its residents. In fact, he and John had almost become friends before John had encouraged pretty Bernie and her family to spend the previous Christmas in Haven.

John had thought himself clever, timing it all so well. He would spend some time with Bernadette, whom he'd begun to care for a very long time ago but who'd never much noticed him, all the while with the enthusiastic support of his former mentor, Bernadette's uncle, who favored the match. John would show Bernadette his very fine vicarage and the lovely village and when he'd beguiled her with his success, he would propose.

And he had.

And she'd accepted him. It had all been storybook perfect—except that even before he'd had the opportunity to make an impression on the new, adult Bernadette, she'd already unhorsed Lord Matthias into a snowdrift and irrevocably captured his lordship's attention. A momentary encounter on a country road had overturned every single meticulously planned detail of John's courtship.

John hammered more violently for a moment, picturing a certain poaching rake of a lord sitting upon the head of his nail. Then the anger subsided, as it always did, because Matthias wasn't a rake or a poacher. He'd been a man lost in mourning for the wife and child he'd lost tragically several years before. Since he'd come to Haven, John had racked his brain for some way to help Matthias.

Well, John had certainly helped him, by bringing the one person who carried within her a certain spark, a clear, brilliant vitality that shone from her lovely eyes—and yes, with enough experience with her own tragedy to help a broken man move on from his. Bernie had even brought along a new child, her worldly-wise little brother Simon, to brighten the dark halls of Havensbeck.

At the thought of Simon, John put the hammer down and drank a swig of tepid, overly steeped tea. He grimaced at the taste. He couldn't seem to make a decent pot of tea for himself. He ought to go inside and warm himself at the hearth, but the sun was still on the crystalline valley and the days were so short now. He couldn't bear to spend a moment of it indoors.

Young Simon would be climbing the walls on a day like today, wanting to be outside. John felt the same way, edgy and twitching with house-bound restiveness. The sun was bright on the snow and the wind was slight, giving the day a deceptively balmy feel. John had lived in Haven long enough to know better. The ice was thick on the River Churnet and the night would fall black and impenetrable in just a few hours.

John stepped back and looked at his handiwork.

Building things wasn't what he'd been raised to do. His father would likely shudder at the very idea, yet John had found real enjoyment in the use of his healthy body and his new, hard-won skills.

Now, the exterior window frames were entirely complete. Every window had fine new glass and a spacious windowsill. He'd designed deep sills for the single shining memory of young Bernadette curled up on a sunny windowsill of her uncle's vicarage, lost in a book. The sun had glinted on her amber-brown hair and the light had shone into her eyes, making her squint resentfully though she was clearly too enraptured by what she was reading to bother adjusting her position. She'd been no more than a gawky fifteen and he'd been just another boring adult, albeit a young one. She'd been polite to him when she remembered he existed, but she'd never invited him into that personal, clearly magical world behind those eyes.

John had been an awkward and officious twenty, very aware of his own importance as the selected student of the venerated Vicar Goodrich. Young Bernie mocked him politely for his determination to bring God to the world whether the world liked it or not, and Vicar Goodrich had shown him a gentler approach of guidance and support. Vicar Goodrich had led John by example, bestowing grace in constant small doses that brought succor and strength to everyone around him. A new ambition had been born in John, to set aside the fire and brimstone he'd been taught to favor, and instead to serve with generosity and patience.

And to do it with Bernadette Goodrich at his side.

He'd been so relieved when his scrawny, spotty youthful looks had improved and it became likely that a young lady would not be averse to becoming the vicar's wife. John's only hope was that clever, lively Bernie might feel the same.

So close. He'd missed making that impression upon her by a bloody hour!

John sighed and closed his eyes. *You are the vicar.* "I shall not curse." He looked skyward. "Sorry."

The empty house didn't comment. The spacious rooms and the fine new windowsills and the impervious roof simply sat there, offering nothing in return for his hard work.

The feeling gripped him again, that need for action, for desperate occupation so that he could fall exhausted into his cold bed at night and not spend hours imagining the Christmas he might have been having this year with his beloved new family.

One bloody hour.

He ran his hand through his saw-dusted hair and squinted at the bright day once more. He had close to three hours before night fell.

STUPID. BLOODY. ROCK!

John didn't even bother to pronounce his anti-cursing ritual. He was one chunk of sandstone short of a full load in his mule-cart and the small white sun hung so low on the hillside across the river that it looked as if it might roll right down the snowy slope. It was already growing dark in the cut of the river.

He should leave now, if he wished to get the cart home before full dark. He would just have to come back another time for the last stone. It wasn't as if he would even be able to lay the stone on the terrace until spring. Sometimes he doubted his own good sense. Yes, he should definitely go.

Instead he dug his pry bar into the crack between the frozen ground and the large hunk of sandstone he had ambitiously chosen. This was meant to be a cost-saving measure, not a penance. It didn't hurt that it was one less thing he would have to request from his lordship. Matthias would shrug and order the finest flagstones the quarries downriver could cut. Then every time John walked upon them, he would recall that his life and his work was entirely dependent upon the support of the man who had stolen the woman John had set his heart on.

Grunting, John pounded the pry bar deeper with a few strikes of his sledgehammer, then he put all his weight into shifting the rock. The exertion made his cold, tired body ache and his head pound.

For just a bit more strength, he cast his thoughts back to the sight of Bernadette and Matthias, with their coats covering their wedding garb, leaving the Havensbeck chapel to be greeted by every single denizen of Haven, all equally bundled up, who had cast cut paper snowflakes at the sheepishly grinning couple in lieu of flower petals. Bernie, laughing, alight with joy. Matthias, gobsmacked by his own good fortune and most definitely smug about it.

Weeks. Mere weeks of courtship. Bernie had been so mad for Matthias, and he for her, that John had taken the high road and stepped aside—and Matthias hadn't lost a moment in making his conquest.

"*Rraahh!*" Spurred by the twist of the knife of memory, John convulsed his entire body, aiming all his disappointment and fury and hurt at the pry bar—and ripped the wide, flat piece of sandstone from the frozen earth.

As if in answer, a high, feminine scream cut the icy air.

JOHN FOLLOWED THE cry, running along the riverbank, slipping in the snow. Ahead he could see the silhouette of the bridge against the dimming sky and the shadow play of a damaged carriage tilting slowly, slowly over the stone balustrade of the bridge.

The neighing of distressed horses echoed the screams. He kept running, scrambling up the bank now to access the bridge level.

"Hold on!"

More cries from the carriage. "Help! I can't hold her. She's falling!"

John looked up to see a limp form hanging from the carriage that still threatened to topple over the edge of the bridge. Then he realized why. One of the horses had already fallen over the side and was now dangling from its harness, screaming in panic and thrashing wildly. Every convulsion of its giant body tore at the carriage, dragging it down, crushing it against the low stone wall, while the other panicked horse, still on the bridge but fighting the pull with all its might, threatened to rip the vehicle apart with its plunging antics.

The lady in the silk gown hung pale and unmoving except for the limp sway of her upper body as she hung with her lower half and skirt trapped within the carriage.

It only took a split of a second for John to assess the situation and make a decision. He'd never be able to secure the carriage in time, for the dangling horse was doing more damage by the moment. "I'm getting below her! I'll catch her!"

"Hurry!"

John scrambled down the rocky bank and slithered awkwardly out onto the ice until he stood just beneath the insensible lady. She'd slipped a bit farther out of the carriage. The other woman must be losing her grip.

"Now! Let her go!" John cried over the wheezing and groaning of the trapped horse, whose rear hooves whipped the air in alarming nearness to John's upraised arms.

The lady fell silently, with only the flutter of her skirts and cape to mark her descent. As she turned in the air, John had a brief impression of black and white and scarlet before she landed in his arms and knocked him back hard onto the ice. The wind left his lungs in a great whoosh and his arse ached, only partially protected by his thick woolen coat, but he'd caught her!

As he tried to bring any possible scrap of air back into his chest, he looked back up at the carriage to spy wide, worried eyes in a pale face, peering down at him and his catch.

"Get free!" he tried to say. Before he could gather the breath to shout a warning, the harness broke into pieces, the sounds like gunshots as the leather straps rent and the traces snapped—

And the horse fell.

Chapter 2

JOHN WRAPPED HIS arms about the lady and rolled. As he'd feared, the massive crack of the ice behind him marked the horse's impact. He kept rolling, for there was no time to stand and lift and run—

He felt the crack run beneath him, cutting through the ice near his ribcage. The world shifted and rolled and John knew that the ice was shattering beneath them. He scrambled to his knees and grabbed a fistful of silk, crawling desperately toward the bank before the ice broke into floes too small to hold them and they slipped into the deathly river. He might survive it—it was not his first encounter with failing ice—but the injured woman in his arms would sink like a stone, her skirts so heavy with water that she'd not be able to remain above the ice even if she were fully conscious and a strong swimmer.

He grabbed at the ice where it had frozen into raised rivulets and pushed hard with his boots and pulled his charge with all his might. He practically threw her up onto the bank as his trailing feet sank beneath the water and all sensation in his legs ended.

"Emmeline! Em! Oh, wake up Em! Wake up!"

John blinked vaguely up at the person on the bank now kneeling over the unconscious lady. "A hand, madam," he wheezed, "if you do not mind?"

The person crawled toward him, grabbed two fistfuls of his coat and leaned back from the river. This was surprisingly helpful, enabling John to drag himself free of the deadly cold water tugging forcefully at his feet. Clearly the lady was a sturdy sort.

They both turned at a great splashing and snorting to see the fallen carriage horse clambering ashore not far from them. John stared in astonishment, for he'd assumed the beast was doomed by its fall.

Next to him, a voice snarled. "Of course, the idiot creature survived, it being all his fault! Poor Emmeline!"

John turned to examine his helper for the first time. She was very pale, with ruddy blotches of worry and distress upon her cheeks as she gazed down at her unconscious companion. Round-faced and freckled with pale brows and lashes, the worried lady wore a gray woolen cloak over a dark-colored dress.

John looked down at the woman he still held close and the breath left his body at her still pale beauty. The white he'd seen was the ivory of her perfect complexion. The black was her shining hair tumbling over the snow. The startling red was the blood that traced rivulets over her brow and cheek. She was clad in purple silk and her matching cloak was lined in fur.

His pounding heart skipped a beat. She looked like misplaced royalty. As if she'd heard that stuttering pulse, the woman stirred slightly and opened eyes of such a rich and stunning blue that John's mind could only come up with the word "violet".

She blinked up at him, her gaze unfocused and vague. "My...angel," she whispered before her lids fell shut once more.

She was the most beautiful woman John had ever seen.

"You'll both die of chill shortly, so kindly stop mooning over Lady Emmeline before you're so cold that you'll be of no use whatsoever!"

The annoyed tone shook John free from his gobsmacked state. The sharp-tongued woman was entirely correct. He had already lost sensation in his wet feet and the injured lady needed to be seen to immediately.

However, John was not accustomed to being spoken to as if he were nothing more than a foolish servant. Deciding that any reply he might make now would only be something to regret later, he held back his retort and clambered awkwardly to his numb feet.

Getting the unconscious beauty up the slick, snow-covered bank required cooperation, which brought about more caustic commentary from the gray-cloaked woman. Repressing his irritation in favor of saving lives, as any gentleman would do, John followed the woman's snarled orders until they reach the high point of the bank and were able to follow the snowy lane. The woman then ran ahead to where the carriage still canted dangerously over the low stone wall of the bridge.

"Mr. Higgins? Mr. Higgins!" The woman flung herself forward, skidding to her knees on the packed, trampled snow and crawling beneath the carriage.

Foolish female! With his arms full of his own rescue, John could do little to stop the lady's companion from endangering herself. Then he saw that she scooted backward out of the space beneath the spinning wheels with her fists full of someone's burly arm. The missing driver!

She glared at John over her shoulder as she tugged. "Oh for pity's sake! Just go lead the horse onward for a few yards, so I can get to Mr. Higgins properly!"

John moved to do just that. The second horse, still mostly in its harness, was somewhat the worse for wear than its companion who now clopped wearily along the bridge toward them, having followed John. The still-harnessed horse stood bracing its own weight against the pull of the tilting carriage, its hide covered in sweat, with foam forming around its bit. The creature was clearly in great distress.

With his arm full of woman, John could just about free one hand to grab the trailing rein. "Come along, lad. Shh. All is well. Quiet."

The horse rolled him a disbelieving eye, but responded with a small reluctant step when John let him onward. The carriage shuddered. Another step, and another. The carriage teetered.

"Beware!" John called back over his shoulder, his voice muffled by the folds of the lady's cloak piled against his neck. He ought to put her down, but where? She was so cold already it hardly seemed a good notion to lie her down on the snow.

"Come along," he urged the horse. "Just a step, lad. Just another step."

The carriage creaked mightily, then noisily scraped forward, one side still angled out over the wall. Another step and another, until John heard the gray-cloaked woman cry out.

"We are clear!"

Which was a good thing, for the carriage suddenly fell back upon its four wheels with a crash. The impact collapsed it like a house of cards, turning it to naught but a pile of lacquered firewood.

Oh damn. John released the horse and staggered back to check on the lady's companion and the driver.

Rounding the wreckage, he was stunned to see the woman crouching over the injured man, clearly shielding his body from the debris still falling from the tilted top of the carriage. John gasped to see a large wooden trunk begin to slide directly toward the two on the snowy ground.

There was no time to put the lady down, even had there been a place to put her. With his hands full, all John could do was to thrust his body into the path of the sliding trunk and take the impact on his back and shoulders.

Ouch.

Such a day he'd had.

Deflected by mere flesh and bone, the trunk slithered safely away to fall a few feet past the driver and the lady's companion. Grudging admiration filled him. Annoying as the woman might be, John had to admit she took little care for herself when someone else was in need.

More things rained down upon John's back, baskets and bundles and lightweight hat boxes. He took the small bumps without complaint, but when something burst open and showered him with dainty underthings, John's long-suffering silence shattered.

"Bloody damned *hell!*" He bellowed. He shook his head violently to dislodge something lacy and smelling of lavender water. It only fell down to encircle his neck like a clerical collar.

The driver and the lady's companion were staring up at him in openmouthed shock. Well, that was regrettable. He shook his head. *So sorry.*

John heard voices and looked to see damned Matthias and—oh, but of course!—Bernadette running up the lane to their aid. The manor was just up the rise. Someone must have heard the ruckus.

John resigned himself to helplessly standing there with an unconscious woman in his arms and a set of lacy drawers around his neck.

A snicker erupted at his side. He cast a glance of loathing at the lady's companion. Rude creature, after all he'd done.

It didn't help that once the two injured people had been sorted into the hands of his lordship's excellent staff, Bernie had looked at John with a twist to her lips that told him she repressed a snicker of her own.

With the entire staff rushing to aid them, John was forced to give up his lovely burden. John would have liked to stride into Havensbeck Manor still carrying his rescued lady, making quite the heroic picture. However, there was no denying that during the evening's adventure he'd done something rather awful to his back muscles. He staggered into the great house like a bent old man, bracing himself on door jambs and furniture until he could collapse onto a sofa. It was all he could do not to whimper out loud.

The house's greater concern was for the lady and the driver. Lady Emmeline had a head injury and was unconscious. Mr. Higgins, who had been trapped between the stone side wall of the bridge and the carriage, had suffered a dislocated shoulder and several cracked ribs.

All this John found out when the physician had finished with the injured two and someone—probably Bernie, since John was fairly certain that Matthias thought of him as little as possible—sent the man in John's direction.

"You've pulled a few muscles in your back, lad. Got off lightly, you did. Best to go on home and rest yourself."

Since he could manufacture no excuse to stay, John rubbed his stiffening back and prepared to leave Havensbeck for his vicarage. He would have liked to check in on Lady Emmeline with the otherworldly violet eyes. He even thought to search out the horses, the silly falling one and the brave stalwart one, but it grew very late and it was a long cold walk home.

At the unattended front door, John stopped short. What of his mule? Was the poor thing still standing on the riverbank harnessed to the cart full of stones?

"John?"

Bernadette. John steeled himself to turn toward the woman he'd waited six years to marry.

She looked every inch the lady of the manor she floated toward him with a swish of expensive skirts. She smiled up at him. "You're not leaving now. It's half-past ten and you're exhausted. You're staying here tonight."

It was not a request, or even a demand. Bernie declared it a fact and John, as ever, could refuse her nothing.

"But my mule—"

"Is in the stable, enjoying a hot mash along with Lady Emmeline's carriage horses." She smiled up at him warmly. "All is well and collected, even Lady Emmeline's baggage." Her lips twitched and John knew he was never going to hear the end of Lady Emmeline's lacy drawers. John could only smile back hesitantly. *Oh, Bernie.*

"I must ask you, John," came the deep voice of Lord Matthias from the shadows of the foyer, "whatever were you doing digging stones in the middle of winter?"

John very carefully did not draw back guiltily from Bernadette, for they were doing nothing more than having a conversation. Alone. In the darkened foyer. Bernadette was only being a good hostess, and a good friend. They were not standing particularly close. The moment of intimacy was entirely of John's own imagining.

Or perhaps not, by the steely glint in Matthias's eyes as the lord of the manor stepped into the candlelight.

You've won, John glared back. *Let it go.*

Matthias's gaze narrowed. *I will when you do.*

Bernadette clapped her hands sharply. When both men turned startled expressions upon her, she scowled at them. "If you're finished with your masculine posturing, my love, will you see to our guest? Since you seem somehow dissatisfied with my own actions?" She tilted her head at her glowering husband and smiled so sweetly that John, knowing Bernie well, rather feared for the poaching bastard.

Not a poacher. Not a bastard.

Bernie had a right to choose anyone she liked, and Bernie had chosen Matthias.

Let her go. Think of something else, for pity sake!

The acerbic tone in his own mind made John think of the lady's companion. He didn't know her name. "Ah, what is Lady Emmeline's condition? "

Bernie's expression saddened. "She is still unconscious, poor girl. It seems she struck her head on the stone wall as she was flung out the carriage door. If it had not been for Miss Grey's quick thinking, she'd surely have fallen to her death on the ice!"

Miss Grey had saved the day, had she? All by herself?

THAT BUMBLING DOLT!

Miss Norah Grey gently bathed Emmeline's forehead with a dampened cloth. Em didn't have a fever, but her poor head had taken such a knock that Norah felt it couldn't do any harm.

That idiot, flinging himself—and Emmeline!—into the path of

that falling trunk! Norah flinched again, recalling how the solid wood had narrowly missed Emmeline's skull as it glanced off the stupid fellow's thick shoulder.

She knew her anger was irrational, but anger at a stranger seemed a safer direction for her thoughts than remembering the accident. Her memory skidded away from those appalling moments even then. It was easier to blame the man on the bridge than to acknowledge her own failure.

A faint tap at the bedchamber door preceded their hostess, Lady Bernadette, who entered with fresh candles and an efficiently bustling maid.

"I thought you might like to catch a bit of rest, Miss Grey. Higgins will be happy to care for Lady Emmeline for a while."

"No, I—" Norah looked at the maid curiously. "Higgins? Like our driver?"

"My brother, miss," the pretty maid answered. "His lordship himself hired him up from London. Factory work had done my brother ill and I asked milady if we couldn't find something a bit more healthy for him up here in Staffordshire."

Norah blinked. "Healthy? Oh dear."

Lady Bernadette grinned, her smile wide and mischievous. "Oh, don't fret. The physician said he'll be fine in a month, though he'll have a weather-ache in that shoulder. Right now he has half the maids in the house vying to rub a bit of liniment on his... ah... heroic vainglory."

"That's thanks to you, miss," Miss Higgins added with a curtsy. "And he's right besotted now, for it. Miss Grey this and Miss Grey that!" Miss Higgins sent a saucy wink at Norah, who bit her lip in amusement.

"I see. Well, I must give... oh, what is the name of the gentleman who assisted us?"

"The vicar? Oh, that would be John Barton."

The vicar? Really? Norah hoped that God wielded a powerful bar of soap for cursing vicars. "Well, the... the vicar did his part. He caught Emmeline in his arms when she fell from the bridge height—"

"He what?" Lady Bernadette stared at Norah. "Christmas bells!"

Norah decided she liked Lady Bernadette a great deal. Quite frankly, she hadn't expected to do so. When she'd learned of Lord

Matthias's invitation for Christmas, she'd worried that the new wife might not appreciate the reminders of the old wife.

Six months past, Lord Matthias's man of business had simply walked up the stairs at Kewell Abbey and stoutly declared that after years of searching the branches of the family tree of Lady Marianna of Havensbeck Manor, the heiress had been found at last. Lady Emmeline Grey, poor daughter of a destitute baron, had received a lavish fortune and a standing invitation to visit Havensbeck Manor at her leisure.

Yet Lord Matthias had remarried. Having the family of your new husband's beloved first wife arrive for an extended visit in the middle of winter? It sounded a bit of a cautionary tale!

Now she could see that Lady Bernadette was only warmly concerned for "Cousin Emmeline".

Norah shrugged. "Well, when the harness broke and the horse fell nearly on top of them and the vicar managed to roll Emmeline out of the ice and onto firm ground—"

Both maid and milady now stared at Norah, agog.

Norah frowned. "Why? What did the vicar say happened?"

Lady Bernadette shook her head slightly. "He said you were very brave and saved both Cousin Emmeline and poor Higgins."

It was Norah's turn to go wide-eyed. "But I didn't! Well, I suppose I—but Emmeline might be dead if not for him."

Lady Bernadette sat back with her arms folded and a cross wrinkle between her brows. "Hang you, John Barton!"

Miss Higgins dusted her hands together. "Now, miss. Let's get you into a nightdress and into bed. You had a ragged sorta day, I'll wager."

Norah opened her mouth to protest that she'd rather stay with Emmeline, but her weary thoughts were no match for Miss Higgins in a zealous bout of efficiency. She found herself tucked in, having been benevolently forced into a quick wash, a hair brushing and braiding, a very luxurious winter nightdress and a wide soft bed in the chamber down the hall from Emmeline's.

Having submitted thus far, she hadn't the mustard to resist the weight of her own drooping eyelids. With only a moment of imagining the tall, brawny vicar snatching Emmeline out of thin air, Norah fell asleep as if she'd been bespelled.

JOHN, HAVING HAD his concerns addressed and knowing that pacing the floor all night over Lady Emmeline's condition wouldn't do a thing to alleviate her danger, forced himself to have a quick wash, accept and don a very luxurious nightshirt—probably belonging to Matthias for it was a good match in size—and lay down upon a bed too wide and soft by far.

Tomorrow he'd have a word with the conniving lady's companion about her tendency to aggrandize herself. Not in a competitive manner, no. More that it was his duty to redirect the path of the selfish onto a way more honorable.

Her mistress, now—there was the very face of graciousness.

So beautiful, he mused sleepily. Really so very lovely, with those improbable violet eyes.

The way she gazed up at him, so wistfully. "My angel," she had called him. Then she had been silent again, so silent and still.

Chapter 3

WAKING UP IN a sumptuously appointed bedchamber in Havensbeck Manor was most disconcerting. Norah blinked at the unfamiliar fall of rose-colored jacquard curtains surrounding the vast bed in which she slept. This rather pleasant fog of extravagance only lasted until Norah recalled poor Emmeline.

With a gasp, she flung back the covers and sprang from the bed. Miss Higgins must have worked as quietly as a mouse, for all Norah's gowns were hanging, cleaned and pressed, in the wardrobe, even the one she'd worn the day before.

It seemed a year since she and Emmeline had jotted off early from the inn, but it had been only yesterday morning!

It was just past sunrise, so Norah turned to close her bedchamber door quietly as she left. Thinking of Em, she whirled to rush down the hallway.

And ran into a large masculine wall.

"Oof!"

Large masculine hands caught her as she stumbled back from her collision with a large masculine chest.

"Oh damn!... I mean... My deepest apologies, Miss Grey!"

It was the cursing vicar who had run her down like a careening ale cart. Of course.

She staggered and his grip tightened to steady her. "Oh heavens, I am fine. Yes, yes, now kindly get off!" She prepared to heft him a decidedly unladylike shove if he didn't let go, but he released her at last.

Holding back a snort of disdain with all her might, more out of respect for the collar than the man, Norah impatiently tugged her bodice straight. It seemed her neckline had caught hold of his top coat button, gifting the vicar with a view of rather more of her bosom than she'd ever intended. She hoped he hadn't spotted it. The way he looked swiftly away proved he had indeed noticed.

With a withering glare that she really couldn't restrain, she bustled off impatiently muttering under her breath. That man!

He did smell very nice though.

VICAR JOHN BARTON stood gazing after the woman whose collision with him had made him feel as though he were on the losing side of a pillow fight. Then, she'd snarled at him again. Now he was certain the words "clumsy ox" had drifted back down the hall to his ears.

That woman!

The fact that she treated him so rudely didn't seem to matter to his physical body, which had very much enjoyed the forceful impact of the lady's generous anatomical differences. The flash of the sumptuous tops of her breasts didn't help.

Give me strength.

Miss Grey disappeared into Lady Emmeline's chamber down the hall, which was precisely where John had been headed. He'd wished to check on the lady's condition before he went down to breakfast.

Rethinking the matter, John decided he ought to take his gullible body out for a brisk walk in the cold air, just to teach it some discernment. Then he would feed it some ham and eggs and hopefully they could put the entire incident behind them.

The body had a point, however. It was high time the vicar took a wife.

His chest ached. He would have, if that poaching bastard hadn't taken her first.

He sighed. "My apologies, Lord."

I shall not curse.

"LADY EMMELINE IS the heiress to Lady Marianna's estate, found at long last," Lady Bernadette told John as she leaned back in her chair at the breakfast table with her second cup of tea. "Of course, Matthias never thought she'd leap at his invitation, not when she would have to travel in such snow. But she and her relations are most welcome. They are Marianna's family, so they are Matthias's and mine now as well."

She spoke very naturally of her husband's beloved first wife, who had died along with his small son in a fire long ago. It seemed Bernie had come to terms with that lost love and felt secure in Matthias's new but unshakable love for her.

John was surprised. "A matrilineal entailment? That's unusual."

She nodded. "But it is done—and by heaven it ought to be done more often!" Bernie tossed back her tea and then unsuccessfully hid a catlike yawn. "Oh dear. I was up so late—and I've so much to do today!" She sighed and stood, waving John back to his seat with a newly acquired social grace. It suited her, this new mantle of Lady of the Manor.

Although personally quite informal, Bernadette Goodrich had been born a lady and had lived the life of a well-bred girl until the death of her and young Simon's parents in her fourteenth year. As the wards of a poor vicar and his hardworking wife, Bernie and Simon had been well cared for, but it had been no life of luxury, rather grim and sparse. Becoming Lady Bernadette was more a matter of remembering herself than transforming into someone altogether new.

She was now clearly deliriously happy, despite her frantic attention to the holiday preparations. Miss Bernie Goodrich, now turned Lady Bernadette of Havensbeck Manor.

Her green eyes twinkled at him now and old pain tugged somewhere in his chest. Bernie had been the one for so long. Now she was someone else's one.

Let her go.

John wasn't sure how that was to be done. He had checked the Book, which had never failed him before. Sadly, it only instructed him not to covet. It didn't explain how to stop coveting. Should he enact some hedge-witch ritual, like waving a pair of shears over his heart under a full moon to symbolically snip an invisible thread?

Lady Bernadette dashed from the room, fully energized despite her alleged weariness. John had no doubt she would finish all her tasks and they would be done with love.

Oh, Bernie.

Then she popped her head back into the breakfast room—which was more luxurious than many a dining room—and lifted one finger.

"And Miss Grey is not Lady Emmeline's lady's companion. She is her cousin, through their fathers. So no inheritance for poor Miss Grey. If I were Miss Grey, I would be green with envy, wouldn't you?"

With an affectionate little wave, she disappeared again.

Should he tell her that her fondness and friendship actually made it worse? *Never.*

Still, her last comment explained a great deal.

Caustic Miss Norah Grey seemed to have fallen prey to envy. Her cousin had beauty and high standing, now considerable wealth as well—and Miss Grey had none of that. Miss Grey might be forgiven for her unlikable disposition, but John wasn't in a particularly forgiving mood at the moment.

Blast that woman! He sighed and looked heavenward. *I know, I know.*

NORAH FROWNED AT Miss Higgins. "Why ever should I allow that man to sit with Lady Emmeline? This is her bedchamber!"

"He's the vicar, miss! Shouldn't he ought to be looking after the poor little one's soul?" Miss Higgins looked down. "Just ... in case, like?"

Norah did know. In case.

In case Emmeline never woke.

Norah tightened her fingers around Em's limp hand in hers. It was all her fault that Em was in this fix! If only she'd done more to restrain Emmeline's impulsive urge to race on toward the manor in her stylish new carriage.

It was clear from the beginning of the four-day journey that Emmeline felt restricted by the pace required by the elder members of their party in the second carriage. When she'd learned that their destination lay yet another day away at their snail's pace, she'd been frantic to fly onward to her brilliant new destiny.

What would another day of travel have really cost? Much less than had speeding on those snowy roads, fanned onward by Emmeline's giddy impatience!

For most of her very attractive life, no one had been able to deny Emmeline anything. It was a tribute to Em's naturally sweet disposition that she wasn't a holy terror by this, her nineteenth year.

As it was, Emmeline had been able to wheedle even Norah into yesterday's unwise adventure—and Norah had believed herself to be entirely immune to her cousin's ebullient charm.

Yet you did say yes, and you even helped her sneak out the baggage so silently in the predawn light. Now Emmeline was going to die.

It is all your fault!

Quelled by her guilt and overwhelming grief at the very thought of Emmeline coming to such an early and unnecessary end, Norah swallowed her objections and nodded jerkily at Higgins to let the vicar in.

The dratted cursing vicar! Of all people to take innocent Emmeline's soul into his hands!

Of course, Nora must give him his due. He had saved Emmeline from a terrible fall. The way Emmeline had hung out over the frozen river—and the way Norah's grip had begun to slip—

Vicar Barton entered and, with a short nod of acknowledgment, he sat opposite Norah. The two of them became as still and silent as cast-iron bookends framing the pale unconscious beauty on the bed.

Norah barely looked up from Emmeline's hand in hers. It always been Norah's one small vanity that she had pretty hands, graced with long elegant fingers. Yet Emmeline's were still prettier. Norah didn't care. She held Em's more lovely hand with every ounce of will inside her directed at the pale flicker of life within her cousin. *You will be fine, Emmeline. You will be just fine.*

The incredibly annoying vicar stirred on the other side of the bed. His slight movement wafted his scent across the still, silent room. He did not smell of heavy cologne or sickly perfumes. Rather, it reminded Norah of the pine forest under a freshly fallen snow.

She had caught that scent just this morning. That distracting encounter in the hall outside her chamber had left her skin tingling from the unaccustomed contact. She wished she could say that the memory gave her a shudder of revulsion, but she was not so dishonest with herself. Her senses had flared to life, as if hungry for more such enticement.

It was no matter, simply a natural animal reaction to an acceptable male in a female animal's vicinity. Well, rather more than acceptable.

He was handsome, if one liked men who were tall, broad-shouldered, with dark blond curling hair and eyes the color of pewter.

Oh, I cannot bear myself right now!

Here she sat with Emmeline's very possibly dying hand held in hers, yet she had the callousness to think about "eyes the color of pewter" and "a pine forest under a freshly fallen snow"! Her huff of self-loathing caught Vicar Barton's attention and he gave her a quizzical look.

The very color of pewter. The polished and cherished kind, like some plate or pitcher held as an heirloom from a beloved relation.

She was so revolted by her own ill-timed attraction that she lifted her chin to glare back at him. He was the source of her inappropriate but undeniable interest. So what if he was handsome? He wasn't the first handsome man she'd seen. Emmeline and Norah, as her chaperone, spent their afternoons and evenings surrounded by hopeful suitors, some of whom were held to be very good-looking fellows, although Norah had never really thought so.

The man before her was far more appealing than the silk-clad peacocks that swarmed to Emmeline's side, even in his coarse farmer's shirt and simple trousers. Norah did not deny the lure. However, this man's effortless good looks and rather riveting natural scent need have nothing to do with her. He was just some country vicar, one she'd likely never meet again after this holiday.

A rather heroic country vicar, remember?

Again, that had nothing to do with her world, her life, or her future. She had long understood that she would never marry.

She was too plain and too outspoken to catch the notice of a wealthy gentleman and too destitute to tempt a poor one. It didn't matter. From the outside looking in, Norah didn't really see the advantage to marriage for a woman. All that wooing seemed to go away once the wedding ended, and when the necessary procreation was complete, the women of Norah's acquaintance seemed to think very little about their husbands except as arbiters of their spending money.

However, Norah did like children. She'd always counted on Emmeline having a handful of them, and then Norah could be part of their little lives.

Dotty old Cousin Norah pottering around in her attic room, dusting her fusty old books and hoping another woman's child will drop in for a game of draughts.

Sometimes Norah's inner voice was rather unkind. It was a flaw she meant to work on, very soon.

Emmeline's hand lay cold and still in hers and she felt a pang of further mourning within her overwhelming misery. If she lost Em, she would also lose her own future as part of Emmeline's family. No one else needed Norah the way Emmeline did.

Her cousin would make a loving, careless parent, full of spontaneous fun and unpredictable thoughtfulness, but she had always planned on having Norah's help with the serious matters of running a household and child-rearing.

Emmeline, if you wake up, I will choose all your staff for you from the scullery to the governess. I will surround you with good, stable people who will steer your life well and never take advantage of your sweet nature.

Norah felt anger well up inside her at the thought of some conniving butler skimming from the household budget, or worse, some horrendous child nurse punishing Emmeline's little one too cruelly—

"Are you unwell, Miss Grey?"

JOHN CRINKLED HIS brow at Miss Grey's furious glare that seemed to be directed at nothing in particular. "Miss Grey, has someone done something to displease you?"

She broke her deadly intensity to blink at him in confusion. "The governess," she blurted. Then she blushed hotly.

There were no children at Havensbeck but young Simon, who had an excellent young tutor by the name of Eddington Finch, who was currently visiting his family in the next county.

"There is no governess in Havensbeck Manor, Miss Grey. Might this person be a housemaid?" He hardly thought any of the staff of Havensbeck could arouse such ire. Then again, Miss Grey seemed to despise John himself so one could hardly abide by the judgment of such a wildly irrational person.

Miss Grey looked down at Lady Emmeline's pale hand in her own grasp. John was astonished to see a tear drip from the woman's nose. At last, a natural reaction to the terrible situation!

"Do you ever..." Her voice was low and husky now, and surprisingly melodious once done with snapping and snarling.

She trailed off, but John had a great deal of practice coaxing the inner thoughts from stoic country people. He simply waited, his expression serene and only mildly expectant. Eventually his patience bore fruit.

"Do you ever imagine a thing that has not actually happened—and the very idea of it upsets you so severely that you feel very real emotions in the picturing of it?"

John bit back a rueful smile. "On occasion, I do." Virtually every time he caught sight of the former Miss Bernadette Goodrich, actually. "I try not to think too much of it, for it is merely the sign of an excellent imagination, don't you think?"

She stared at him then, her eyes wide and her lips slightly parted. "Do you think so?"

Then she scowled and John remembered that he wasn't particularly fond of this woman.

"That cannot be all that is. I'm positive it says something very dire about my flawed personality that I could be filled with rage at a nonexistent governess."

John almost laughed out loud, but caught his clergyman's practiced dignity about him like a concealing cloak. "I am certain that it is so. Tell me, what has this figment of your imagination done to rile you so?"

She looked away. "I imagined Emmeline's children someday."

Emmeline's children? Not her own?

"And I thought how awful it would be if some nurse or governess was unkind or cruel—"

"Ah. Well, it does happen, I suppose. So you were preparing yourself for dealing with this treacherous person?" She might be a wee bit mad, but at least her irrational fury was in the service of good.

Unlike your own.

She must have caught a flicker of that thought in his expression, for she narrowed her gaze. Miss Grey's focused attention was a bit disconcerting. John felt sorry for the nonexistent governess—that is, until he remembered what she had done—or would do—or neither, for she did not exist!

Dear Lord, she's contagious!

"You really do know what I mean, don't you? Why is that? Why is it that you, of all people—"" She rolled her eyes skyward.

John's irritation began to stir once more.

"*You* should grasp what no one in my acquaintance, nor even in my own family has ever understood?"

I shall not curse. I shall not curse.

"Miss Grey, perhaps we ought to remain peaceful and soothing for Lady Emmeline's sake." It was an unworthy jab, but John was disturbed by more than Miss Grey's scorn.

The fact was that he'd almost liked her for a moment, truly liked her with a flash of that particular joy one feels when meeting someone of like mind and humor, someone whom one instantly recognizes as being important. Someone who could become a true friend.

Despite having earned the respect of the village and being held in mostly good regard by its lord, John's only real friend was Simon, a nine-year-old boy who had almost become a brother, almost a son.

He was also fairly certain that his mule liked him a little bit.

Somehow, he didn't think his little list of recommendations would endear him to the tart-tongued Miss Grey.

His reminder of Emmeline had instantly quelled her prickly moment and she now turned her attention back to her cousin's welfare.

John realized that the entire exchange had taken place in the lowest of tones, almost whispers. With Miss Grey so occupied, John examined her closely. She looked much the same as she had after their collision earlier this morning, pallid and slightly mussed. Her hand trembled as she soothed her cousin's brow. Suspicion stirred within him.

"Have you had breakfast?" Now it was his turn to glare at her. "Be truthful—when did you last eat something?" It was nigh unto luncheon already!

She merely waved a hand at him without looking up from Lady Emmeline. "Miss Higgins brought me a bit of soup last night."

John noticed that she did not claim to have consumed this alleged soup. "And before that?"

She shrugged, an awkward rejection of his concern. "Emmeline was in a hurry to leave for the manor."

"You haven't eaten for two days?"

She looked up at his insistent tone. "We were driving so fast. I don't like a full stomach on such a jouncing pace—"

John was on his feet in a flash. He yanked open the chamber door. "Jasper!"

Oh, that woman!

Chapter 4

A FTER THE INTERFERING vicar had called down upon her the full force of the manor's very determined staff, Norah had found herself fed to near lethargy. Then, when she'd been caught yawning by the eagle-eyed Miss Higgins, she'd been put to bed like a toddler for a midday nap.

It didn't help Norah's protests that she fell asleep at once and did not stir until a ruckus arose in the hallway outside her chamber. A narrow seam of light passing into her curtained bed told her that it was well into the afternoon and the lilting wispy voice wailing in the hallway informed Norah that the rest of her family had arrived.

Sudden cowardice made her want to hide out under the coverlet a bit longer. After all, she was supposed to watch over Emmeline! Despite the fact that she was a scant two years the elder, no one— including Norah herself—had any doubt that it should be the way of things. Norah was clever and more wise about people and the world. Also, Norah had nothing better to do.

Emmeline was never expected to be sensible. Emmeline's primary tasks had always been to be beautiful, to be as fashionable as her formerly limited budget allowed, and to make herself as irresistible as possible to men.

Fortunately, Emmeline enjoyed her work—and Norah would be the first to admit her cousin was very, very good at it. Further, since Em now had a surprise inheritance, she had become not only fashionable but was destined to be a true trendsetter under the tutelage of the great Lementeur, mantua maker to the highest of the high.

I am a terrible guardian, letting Em maneuver me into slipping out early and driving so fast.

She would have to face the family sooner or later. Then she thought of their vast grief at seeing Emmeline in her death – like sleep. Oh goodness, she must hurry!

Norah didn't need a lady's maid to get in and out of her practical gowns. She needn't do more than twist up a quick braid to speak to her own family, so she was out of her bedchamber in mere minutes.

JOHN HAD NEVER been so happy to see Miss Grey as when she entered Lady Emmeline's sitting room.

Emmeline's father, Lord Bester, Baron of something or other, was threatening John with dire happenings if he didn't allow a father see his own daughter, while the elderly duo of ladies seemed inclined to trade off weeping and fainting. One kept crying out the word "naughty." It seemed that some idiot had carried tales of Lady Emmeline's accident far and wide, exaggerating matters greatly, not that matters weren't deadly serious in the first place.

Lord Bester carried on, uttering garbled madness regarding sabotage, highwaymen—and incredibly!—heiress–eating wolves.

John had waited it out, stolidly blocking the doorway to Lady Emmeline's sickroom until someone sane arrived.

It seemed that Miss Grey would have to do.

"Uncle Bester! Stop browbeating the vicar at once!"

For a moment, John thought Miss Grey would actually clap her hands like a schoolmistress at her various relations. Yet her scolding tone worked a treat and the "naughty" woman subsided into gulps of fading hysteria.

Miss Grey came to stand next to John. He felt ridiculously gratified by her support.

Until she opened her mouth, of course.

"Vicar Barton," she turned on him with flashing eyes. They were pretty eyes up close, really, such an interesting blend of green and brown...

He cleared his throat. "Yes, Miss Grey?" *Beware, mate. This one has teeth.*

"Is there a reason—any valid reason at all—that you are keeping my uncle from seeing his own daughter in her time of need?"

Right then. Teeth indeed. "Why no, Miss Grey. We were merely waiting for you to wake from your afternoon nap to join us." With that tiny dig, he bowed himself out of the fracas and sidled around the crowd. There were only four Greys in the room, yet a moment ago it had felt like an invading horde.

As he made his escape, John could hear Miss Grey setting things to rights behind him. "Uncle Bester, you and Great Aunt Blythe should go in first. Mama, you may sit out here with me. Let's have a cup of tea..."

Once outside Lady Emmeline's rooms, John came face to face with Lady Bernadette and Lord Matthias.

Bernie tilted her head. "Coward."

"Sayeth the one hiding in the hall," John retorted. *Too familiar.* He bowed. "My lady."

"You could have handled that better," grumbled Matthias.

John's spine stiffened. That was simply too much. "Then it is a good thing I'm on my way out. Do enjoy your family party. I have a great deal to do at the vicarage." He didn't, actually, but he stomped away in a bitter hurry without tossing in the customary "my lord." He didn't regret it one little bit.

He heard Bernie's soft voice behind him. "That was rude, dear."

"Sorry, my love," Matthias murmured.

That tender reply entirely drained away John's satisfaction over his reckless omission of his lordship's due courtesy. No matter what, Matthias would always win. Had already won, until death did they part.

Oh, Bernie.

NORAH GRIMACED TO herself. She had probably offended the cursing vicar. Well, no matter. She was forever offending someone with her outspoken ways.

Beside her, Mama sniffled. "Oh Nottie, I was so dreadfully worried."

Norah's mood eased. "That's very sweet of you, Mama, but I'm absolutely fine." She felt very well indeed after her feast and her nap, not that she would ever admit it to that dratted man.

"Oh yes, dear. Of course you are. You're always fine. But poor Emmeline!" Mama leaned closer. "What will we all do without her inheritance?"

At least Mama had the grace to whisper such an unworthy question. Norah knew her great-aunt and uncle feared the same.

Naturally, Emmeline was loved by them, each in their own way. Yet primarily Emmeline was *valued.* She was the family's only financial asset, even before Lord Matthias's man had knocked on the door of the historically-relevant-yet-now-crumbling Kewell Abbey to offer deliverance in the form of a far-flung inheritance.

The first time Norah had seen the Abbey at the not-very-discerning age of eleven years, she thought it the grandest place on earth and her cousin Emmeline the lovely princess of a rich kingdom.

Lord Bester had seemed the very picture of a gracious monarch when he had welcomed his younger brother's widow and daughter with casual benevolence.

"It will be good for Emmeline to have a playmate of our own class," he'd said to Norah. He'd meant it kindly enough. Unlike his father, Bester didn't care if his brother had married "down."

The Dowager Baroness, Great-Aunt Blythe, took a shine to Mama and made her "milady's companion." Mama had security for as long as Great-Aunt Blythe lived, as much as anyone at deteriorating Kewell Abbey had security. The place was largely unlivable, with entire wings blocked off where the damp had ruined the walls.

Little Norah and little Emmeline got on very poorly at first, until Norah understood that Emmeline was to be indulged completely. Yet when Em's extremes drew disagreeable attention, it was always Norah who was blamed.

Realizing at last that no reasonable adult resided within fifty miles of the Abbey, Norah took it upon herself to sit on Emmeline until the spoiled little beast desisted. After that they got on famously. Emmeline continued to be overindulged and Norah continued to sit on her when her behavior threatened to become too poisonous.

Norah hadn't had to sit on Em for years. Merely mentioning it was usually enough.

I should've sat on her in that inn yesterday morning. I should have plunked myself right down on her lap before I ever let her talk me into adventuring out on our own.

Now Mama's whispered question came back to haunt Norah.

What would she do if Emmeline did not survive? Who was she if not Emmeline's guardian and guide? Worse, who was she without her sweet cousin and dearest only friend?

Norah squelched that terrible thought instantly. Emmeline would always need her. Only if her pretty cousin managed to secure someone truly stable and goodhearted could Norah imagine a life where she wouldn't be essential. He would have to be someone tolerant and kind, someone who would firmly curb Emmeline's excesses while indulging her harmless and entertaining frivolity.

Warm gray eyes and a shaggy mop of uncombed hair. Thick muscles filling out a common work-shirt and coat.

It was very odd that she should think of the cursing vicar just then, wasn't it?

JOHN SUSPECTED THAT he had overestimated his mule's affections. The animal kept forcing John into the deep snow on the verge of the lane leading back to Haven. When John would stumble into a thigh-high drift, the mule would try to turn the cart and head back to the luxurious Havensbeck stables.

Quite frankly, John didn't blame the beast. The vicarage would be cold and painfully quiet after the holiday bustle of the manor. "It isn't as though you are hauling rocks," he grumbled. Those had been unloaded from the cart and left by the side of the river where they would likely wait until spring.

"My tutor said that in Russia they eat bad mules."

John looked up from stomping the caked snow from the canvas gaiters wrapped around his lower legs to see young Simon Goodrich grinning impudently at him from a seat on the fieldstone wall lining the lane.

I am wearing my vicar suit everywhere I go from now on. He'd lost all authority in his rough work shirt and his canvas trousers. "Everywhere," he muttered at his bad mule. "Possibly even the bath."

To Simon, he tipped his cap. "Master Simon."

Simon rolled his eyes. "Master of a lot of snowy nothing."

Simon, being Bernadette's brother and no real heir to Lord Matthias, enjoyed the benefits of manor life and a lordly education, but owned nothing in his own name and likely never would. It would be the Army or the Church for Simon, unless he suddenly evidenced a heretofore unknown affinity for scholarly pursuits.

Yes, probably the Army. At least Simon would have the clout to make an officer and not an infantryman. Suddenly sorry for his young friend, John grinned back at him. "I'm off to sand something at the vicarage. Want to help?"

Clearly, Simon didn't really want to pitch in with John's self-inflicted manual labor, but he shrugged listlessly and dropped off the wall to fall in step with John and his suddenly edible mule. The mule seemed to sense a stewpot in his future and stepped lively the rest of the way to the vicarage.

Mrs. Higgins from the village tended the vicarage itself, while a group of volunteer women from the village looked after the church. Mrs. Higgins was a fifty-ish woman from a nearby farm with an energetic stomp and a large collection of her offspring and their offspring living in her snug farmhouse. Some of her grown children were also employed by the manor.

Every Saturday, Mrs. Higgins brought over a large basket of food, as arranged through his lordship. Parsnips from last summer's garden, eggs, a roast or a ham, a few loaves of bread and a hefty half-wheel of Staffordshire cheese wrapped in cloth. John did well enough with cold plates and had even mastered the local oatcake, but he hadn't the slightest idea what to do with his weekly allocation of parsnips. By now a wagon load of parsnips resided in the root cellar. He'd never had the heart to tell Mrs. Higgins that he couldn't actually cook. She would only huff at his incompetence. Then she would cook for him and work even harder than she already did.

Although John felt he was a tidy fellow indeed, Mrs. Higgins didn't hesitate to roll her eyes at some manly housekeeping foible and then apply vigorous means to correct it. In a few hours she could scrub what hadn't seemed dirty, dust what hadn't seemed dusty and smack the living daylights out of every carpet in the house. Normally, a single, youngish vicar with a spacious residence might find himself besieged on a Sunday evening by village ladies bearing cakes and pastries, plying him with savory meat pies and flirtatious glances.

No such lady dared trespass upon Mrs. Higgins's territory. John sometimes thought wistfully that he might not mind fending off a bit of culinary seduction, if it came bearing a cake or a pie.

Now, lighting the stove and digging some tidbits from his pantry, John set an acceptable if somewhat masculine tea table, with hefty slabs of meat, cheese, bread and a small jar of jam.

Simon made no complaints and dug right in. John poured the lad a cup of hopefully not-too-dire tea. He thought he was getting better at it.

No hope there. Simon blew on it for a moment, then took a gulp. He immediately drooled it back into the teacup.

"Too hot?" John asked hopefully.

Simon grimaced. "It's like stewed peat." Then, aware that he'd been rude, he awkwardly backtracked. "But I'm sure some people like it like that."

John sighed. "I cannot figure it out. Do you know how to make tea?"

Simon shrugged. "No. But Bernie does. I can ask her."

"No!" John shook his head firmly. "I will figure it out on my own." Then he scowled. "Do you think Matthias can make tea?"

Simon shrugged, losing interest in the topic. "Why would he, when he can tell Jasper to make it?"

John poured his own tea, for as bad as it was, it was what he had. Were women born knowing how to make tea? He'd wager that Miss Grey could make excellent tea. She'd mock him if she knew he couldn't.

The tea overflowed the cup and scalded John's hand. "Bloody hell!"

Simon snickered. "That's what Uncle Isaiah said when the wagon rolled over his foot."

John was only slightly reassured by the notion that his much-revered mentor had spewed out a curse or two. John couldn't seem to make it through an entire hour at a stretch.

I never cursed before last Christmas. Which was a disconcerting thought, that Christmas should bring about such a flaw in his vicarly foundation. Some things he could happily blame upon Matthias. This one was all his own bloody fault. There, he'd done it again. *Sorry.*

I shall not curse.

John frowned and dabbed at the mess he'd made on the kitchen table with a tea towel. It left a stain on the linen. Mrs. Higgins was going to scold him now. *But it's tea... on a tea towel.*

He could envision Miss Grey rolling her eyes and muttering under her breath. That blasted woman!

At least this time he kept it to himself. It was bad enough to falter, worse to be a poor example to fatherless Simon.

"You should maybe start drinking coffee," Simon said pertly and grinned around the piece of bread in his mouth. When John growled and threw a chunk of cheese at him, Simon laughed and dashed back outside, his boots thumping noisily on the freshly polished floor. "See you at the Christmas Ball, Vicar!"

John grunted as his door slammed. The Christmas Ball, which he could not refuse and which would force him to endure the sight of Bernie whirling around the ballroom in her loving husband's arms all evening long.

Damn it!

Chapter 5

ONCE HE'D WANDERED back across the snowy fields to the manor, Simon Goodrich was bored.

It was a very strange feeling. For as long as he could recall, he'd longed for a few hours to simply play, to climb trees or make a dog chase sticks or battle the village boys in one of their drawn-out snowball wars.

Simon had always worked. Even when he was very little, he could remember feeding chickens and carrying kindling. When the day turned too dark to work, Bernie would teach him his letters and numbers.

Then when he became "Master Simon," it was all lessons and maths and writing. While Simon didn't mind studying old battles, he'd much rather fight in one.

Yet this holiday, for the very first time in his long nine-year life, Simon had nothing to do.

The staff at Havensbeck was too busy to spare him even a bit of conversation. Bernie and his new brother Matthias hardly stood still for three minutes altogether. The stableboys were caught up treating Lady Emmeline's horses for something called "shock" and now John was too grumpy for even a simple game of chess.

Moreover, the house was brimful of lady guests, all clustered around Lady Emmeline's sickbed—or deathbed, depending on which servant delivered the gossip. Simon started to wonder if Christmas was even going to be Christmas this year. If Lady Emmeline did die, they would have to "rethink matters." That's what Bernie had said this morning.

"You see that it wouldn't be right to celebrate Christmas in a house of mourning, don't you, Simon?"

"Yes, I see."

Bernie had made him say it out loud, which was just an adult trick. Now that he'd said it, he'd not be able to complain later when

Christmas turned dark and sad and the village didn't come to feast and dance and eat large pieces of Cook's towering fancy cakes.

Simon walked down the main hallway of the house, the one that led from the front door all the way back to the ballroom stairs. As he walked, head down in a brown study, hands thrust into his trouser pockets, the staff moved swiftly in a complicated dance of preparation. They flowed past him carrying linens and vases, brooms and coal scuttles, always with a "good afternoon, Master Simon" as they passed.

Simon answered politely but automatically, for he was thinking hard.

He was thinking about how it used to be when he and Bernie had lived with Aunt Sarah and Uncle Isaiah. He and Bernie had been closer than close, but Bernie had still been sad much of the time though she'd tried hard to hide it.

It wasn't her new luxurious life at Havensbeck, or the way everyone bowed and called her "milady" that had made Bernie happy. It was Matthias who made Bernie happy.

And vice versa. Simon had learned that term from his tutor and enjoyed using it as often as possible.

Simon's walk slowed further, which seemed to make the servants move faster.

Finally, Simon stopped altogether and stood in the center of the fervor, thinking the right thought at last.

Love.

Love made ladies happy. They became very excited about it, and talked about it, and dreamed about it, like Bernie had when she'd been reading Matthias's messages in the bottles that had been carried down the river, long before she'd ever met him.

Lady Emmeline was sleeping, Bernie had said. An injured kind of sleep, not a good sort. Too deeply, and for too long.

Did Lady Emmeline dream of love in her too deep, too long sleep? Would the dream of love bring Lady Emmeline back if she knew it waited for her in the waking world?

Also, there was John, who was lonely in his nice new house and who couldn't make a decent cup of tea to save his life. John, who still thought about Bernie the way he used to when he was courting her, the way he was supposed to stop thinking about her when she married Matthias. John needed a new lady to think about.

Lady Emmeline was very beautiful, that was the gossip. Rich too, even though John might not care about that.

Very slowly, Simon turned and headed for the grand stair in the front hall.

No one paid him any mind, except for the absent-minded greetings. No one noticed him at all as he wandered slowly into the guest wing, and on down the hallway.

He saw Miss Grey walk out of the sickroom and on down the hall. She left the door slightly ajar, so Simon peeked into the sitting room.

A man—that would be Lord Bester—and a very old lady—that would be the Dowager Baroness—were snoozing in the two chairs by the fire.

Slowly and silently, Simon passed them by.

The bedchamber gave Simon a little pause. Even at his age he knew that a gentleman never entered a lady's bedchamber.

Children did, however. They entered their mothers' and aunts' chambers, didn't they? Wasn't Lady Emmeline family? That's what Bernie had said.

Deciding that facts and tradition lined up in his favor, Simon pushed open the bedchamber door and entered.

There was another lady, not as old as the first one—so that would be Mrs. Grey—but not Lady Grey? Simon feared he would never sort out the peerage. Matthias said he would need to someday. But St. Peter, it was boring!

The lady was snoozing in the chair by the bedside.

Old people snoozed a great deal, didn't they?

In the bed was the famous beauty Lady Emmeline. Simon stopped his slow approach. She didn't look asleep. She looked a little bit dead. That would ruin everything! And also be very, very sad. Yes. Very sad.

Then Simon spotted a slight rise and fall of her coverlet-covered chest and he felt better at once.

Moving to the bedside opposite Mrs. Grey's chair, he bent to the pale beauty's ear and began to whisper.

"SIMON! WHAT ARE you doing here?"

Simon turned to blink innocently at his sister even as he closed

Lady Emmeline's door. Bernie blocked his escape in the hallway and gazed at him with narrowed eyes and fists planted on her hips. Uh-oh.

"I wanted to meet Lord Bester. He's a real baron!" He shrugged. "But they're all asleep. I left."

All true, actually. It was a fine thing to tell the truth and still get away with something. Then he remembered that Bernie was the one who'd taught him how to do that. He eyed his sister warily, but she was too distracted to mind his wording carefully. She blew out a breath that carried a stray lock of hair away from her brow. For a moment, she was the old Bernie, overworked but all his very own.

"Well, you shall have to wait until Lord Bester wants to meet you. We don't introduce ourselves to people of rank. Someone else must do it for us."

Simon shook his head. He was never going to grasp the rules!

"Go on now. I've too much to—"

Simon interrupted her before she could dash away again. "John Barton is really sad, Bernie."

That caught her up, as he known it would. An expression of guilt flashed over her features. Bernie felt bad for what happened with John, even though she had done nothing wrong.

"Did—did he say something to you?"

"I had tea at the vicarage. You should see it. It's really coming along!" Another dig, for the vicarage had been meant for Bernie, but Simon was fighting for Christmas, for heaven's sake! "And he's all alone."

Bernie drew one shoulder back, fidgeting, too uncomfortable to be still. "Simon, you know I—"

"Don't you think with all the ladies here now—don't you think John might like one of them?"

Bernie went very still. Simon knew she was thinking hard. Then she reached out, ruffled his hair, and took off running down the hall toward the main house. Her path intersected with that of Miss Higgins, who carried fresh linens for the bedchambers.

"Higgins, where is his lordship?"

"In his study, my lady."

Dash it, Bernie could still really run, couldn't she?

HOME ALONE, AS usual. John stared unseeing at his cold teapot and the plate of crumbs at Simon's place. He had a fine, finished house and no one with whom to share it. Why should he expect anything to have changed?

Well, you saved a lady from falling to her death on the frozen river. Then you were blamed for the accident. You were able to spend time with Bernie. Then you watched her go all gooey over bloody Matthias. You actually felt a moment of attraction for another woman. Miss Grey's snapping eyes came alive in his memory.

I have had a day.

In the silence, John could hear his mule braying resentfully from the stable. He needed a proper horse.

You need a proper wife. Someone with whom to drink tea and talk about the needs of the village. Someone to remind him to buy a proper horse.

John tried to think honestly of the ladies of his acquaintance. There was Miss Catherine Oglesby, the comely sister of John's best mate in seminary school.

But hadn't Oglesby said in his last letter that Catherine had wed a solicitor and moved to London?

There was Miss Verity Watson, the daughter of the Archdeacon of Cambridge. Then again, John didn't much wish to live in the shadow of the politically calculating archdeacon.

Courting. How was a man supposed to court anyone when he had a village and all of the outlying farms and mines to serve? Matters were quiet now, but come spring he would be so busy wedding and christening his flock that he wouldn't have a moment to leave the village until after the Harvest Festival in October.

He feared he had missed his moment for courtship. All his friends and classmates had gone about it in their early twenties. John had waited for Bernie. He'd felt so above all their whingeing about this lass or that one. He'd made his choice and he'd banked everything on Miss Bernadette Goodrich.

And lost the pot to Matthias.

Knock-knock.

IT WAS MATTHIAS at the door, of all bloody people!

I shall not...

"I've come to invite you to join the—well, party hardly seems the correct word, considering—"

John stared at Matthias. Then a harsh bark of laughter broke from his throat. "Bernie made you come all by your lordly self, did she?" His head swam. He felt drunk on wrath. The simmering resentment of the past year reached some kind of boiling point. John snarled, "Go away."

He abruptly shoved hard at Matthias, and then again, wanting him out of his house, out of his door. Matthias didn't even stagger, as immovable as stone.

As undeniable as lost dreams.

Matthias was always going to be in the way, wasn't he?

Bernie will never love me.

John gasped and backed away from Matthias, shaking his head, trying to reject the single, simple thing he'd managed never to entirely admit to himself.

There had been a lovely young girl, with wise eyes and a warrior's heart, who had so astounded him years ago. Yet suddenly John wasn't even sure if the Bernie he'd loved in his mind all those years wasn't a fantasy Bernie, a creation of his careful, planning nature and his loneliness.

The real Bernie—*Lady Bernadette!*—would never love him, not even if Matthias fell off his beautiful horse tomorrow and left grieving Lady Bernadette all alone.

And it hurt, damn it. The slashing of that strand of his entangled heart bloody well burned.

Matthias—blast him!— seemed to know precisely what was happening. His usually somber demeanor slipped a bit. Pained understanding and sympathy leaked out from the man's jagged edges. The sight jerked John from his spiral of fury and regret.

Oh.

Matthias had needed to do the same thing, hadn't he? He'd had to figure out how to let go, how to reach forward and step out of the bitter past.

"Well hell." John rubbed his face with both hands.

"Bloody hell," agreed Matthias solemnly.

John took a deep breath and let it out, releasing a decade of hopes and dreams and loss. "It had to be you, I suppose?"

Matthias shrugged, a movement that abruptly reminded John of Simon.

Then John looked Lord Matthias of Havensbeck Manor in the eye and saw only a good man, a man who had made his friend Miss Bernadette Goodrich very happy.

John took a breath, and then another.

"Yes, I'll come to Havensbeck."

THEY DIDN'T SPEAK on the way but the silence was not uncomfortable. John and Matthias approached Havensbeck at a walk, an extreme courtesy by his lordship, whose fine gelding could run rings around John's stocky mule and cart.

At least the mule didn't embarrass John by balking. Clearly the animal was eager to reenter the world of heated stalls and steamy oat mash which he so clearly felt he deserved.

Jasper, two gangly young footmen and young master Simon ran out into the snow to greet them several yards from the house.

"The lady! The lady—!" Jasper gasped.

"She's awake!" Simon crowed. "Christmas is back on again!"

NORAH SAT AS close to Emmeline as she could, what with the room full of people. It didn't matter that she was disregarded. Nothing mattered but that Emmeline was all right!

"I have quite the headache, but only that. I really do feel all right." Pale and a little shaky, yet Emmeline was sitting up and smiling.

Miss Higgins, bless her, had no issue commanding Lord Bester to "stop your booming at her, my lord, or I'll have Jasper's lads lock you in your room for the rest of the evening."

Uncle Bester had turned furiously to the lady of the manor lurking in the doorway—for there was no more room in the sickroom!—but when he was met with only bland disregard, he had finally subsided.

Then Miss Higgins, having had the entire story from her brother, spoke quite authoritatively about the accident.

When the proud lady's maid credited her brother for keeping the careening carriage on the bridge, Norah nodded in full agreement.

When Miss Higgins made much of Norah's part in heroically hanging on to the falling Emmeline, Norah only looked away, waving off the admiration. She felt ill at the memory of her own panic and terror, of the grim moment when she realized she was not strong enough to save Emmeline.

Don't let go!

However, when Miss Higgins began to laud the heroism and selflessness of Haven's very own Valiant Vicar, Norah wanted to roll her eyes and leave the room.

Except that every single heroic act Miss Higgins recounted was absolutely and entirely accurate. From this distance it was truly an impressive tale. Mama and Great-Aunt Blythe were practically swooning and even Uncle Bester looked uncharacteristically impressed. Why, the shrewd old fellow was actually misty-eyed at such manly deeds of derring-do.

Norah looked at Emmeline just in time to watch a pale and frightened girl turn into romantically-awed pudding at the tale of her own rescue.

Oh dear. Wait until Emmeline actually saw the man.

Norah tried to intervene in Miss Higgins's account and found herself most assuredly hushed, even by the lady in the doorway. She sat back in her chair in the corner, disgruntled and alarmed for her impressionable cousin.

Yet even Norah had to admit that beneath her panic and worry for Emmeline, something feminine and ageless had taken note of Mr. Barton's thrilling act of heroism. The look on his handsome face, which she had only glimpsed as he ran out onto the ice, had been such an expression of forceful determination. Norah had seen not a thought of fear or even self-preservation in his eyes.

Then John Barton was there, slipping past Lady Bernadette in the doorway and bringing the scent of snow and pine into the room.

Norah felt something catch in her throat at the site of the real Vicar John Barton.

She had only seen him in his rough work clothing. He'd been handsome enough, certainly very manly, but now?

Now he was so clearly the man that everyone in Haven thought him to be. He had a smooth authority, a presence that combined with his handsome face and his kind, warm pewter gaze to make even snobbish Uncle Bester step back in deference.

Oh. I see him now.

A path cleared before the vicar, an open route that led directly to Emmeline, sitting up in the bed in a pool of light from the candles.

Norah was crowded back by her uncommonly deferential relations until she had to stand on tiptoe to gaze over Mama's head.

Emmeline, who looked especially vulnerable and angelic without her usual elegant finish and with her cloud of dark waving hair falling loosely over her enveloping shawl, gazed back at strong, fearless, handsome Mr. Barton as if she'd never before seen a real man.

Considering the feckless, dandified lot that constantly flocked to wealthy, beautiful Emmeline's side, perhaps she had not.

Mama turned to whisper to Great-Aunt Blythe excitedly. She never noticed that she stepped on Norah's toe.

Chapter 6

J OHN QUITE FRANKLY stared. Good Lord, Lady Emmeline was lovely. Really, truly beautiful. Her face was dominated by high cheekbones and her enormous eyes, shining vividly in her still-pale face. Even her lips were perfect, petal pink and full enough to be intriguing in their own right. And all that midnight hair tumbling over her frail shoulders! John found himself quite unable to deny his fascination.

It didn't help matters that she gazed at him as if he stood ten feet tall and slayed dragons every day before breakfast.

John realized that his looks had become more appealing over the years. Unlike Lord Matthias, who'd been darkly handsome every day of his life if one went by the several portraits hanging about the manor, John had been a seedy undergrown sort of boy and then an acne-afflicted young man who'd been left rather scrawny by an unexpected growth spurt at nineteen. Young ladies hadn't been inclined to look his way and even older ladies in his apprenticeship congregation had disregarded his perfectly good guidance because of his unimpressive appearance. He hadn't truly finished maturing until his mid-twenties.

So to have an acknowledged beauty gaze at him so worshipfully was like having his youthful wishes magically granted—intoxicating and somewhat appalling. It made John a little nervous, as if sooner or later Lady Emmeline would scrape off that come-lately layer of socially acceptable looks to find the pimply youth still hidden beneath.

"Oh Mr. Barton, how can I ever repay you for rescuing me from that awful mishap? I should have died on that terrible day if you had not been heaven-sent to catch me!"

John only nodded, not because he meant to be nonchalant but because he'd suddenly lost his ability to speak anything resembling sense. Her wide violet—*yes, violet!*—eyes remained fixed upon his face with adoring attentiveness. She was waiting for something...

Oh yes. "Ah—well, I was working at the riverside, that's all. Anyone would have—I mean, it was the only solution that I could see—"

Her pale cheeks took on a glow. "You are too humble by half, sir. Higgins has recounted how you saved not only me but also her brother and my dear cousin Norah as well!"

It was true enough in its way. His sore back still recounted it every time he pulled on his boots. However, in John's memory the entire affair consisted mostly of landing on his arse in various ways. Clumsy oaf, Miss Grey had called him.

Honestly, this was making him feel uncomfortable. He wasn't interested in hero worship. Yet Lady Emmeline had reached out one elegant hand to him and he took it obediently. At her urging, he sat in the chair at her bedside as close as a relation might, or a lover. Surprisingly, no one objected and soon enough John forgot the small impropriety in the shimmer of those astonishing eyes.

THEY LOOKED MARVELOUS together. They brought to mind a romantic painting with a handsome knight kneeling before a stunning lady.

With a strange sort of recognition, a sense of something clicking into place that had been long awry, there seemed to be a rightness to them together.

Unfortunately, Norah had just realized something very important—but she had realized it just a little bit too late.

I like him.

How could she be so stupid? She was no Emmeline. She wasn't even a tenth as good-looking as Lady Bernadette. Even Miss Higgins outshone her with her pert nose and her impressive figure.

Now that John Barton had seen Emmeline as a woman, not as a object of pity, not an ailing patient, there was no hope his gaze would ever stray to Norah.

No one had ever had to tell Norah she was plain and forgettable. She'd been an observant child and a clear-eyed adult woman. The truth was all around her.

It was in the way gentlemen would look quickly past her. It was in the way everyone, gentleman and ladies both, turned from her to bask in the glow of Emmeline's beauty and effervescent charm. Norah had long been aware that she could choke on a finger sandwich and die dramatically and no one would ever notice as long as Emmeline was in the room.

One by one the family slipped out. Lady Bernadette left her post in the doorway to walk Mama and Great-Aunt Blythe to their chambers.

Norah wasn't supposed to leave the sickroom. She was her cousin's chaperone, placed between Emmeline's beauty and the untrustworthy world.

However, John Barton was as trustworthy as any man Norah had ever known.

Besides, it hurt too much to stay.

JOHN DIDN'T NOTICE that the others had left them alone.

"Tell me about yourself, Mr. Barton. Is it true that you are Haven's own vicar?"

"Not for so very long. This is my first posting as vicar...."

For all her exquisite and rather intimidating beauty, John found it exceedingly easy to talk to Lady Emmeline. She listened most attentively, with her hands clasped before her and her stunning eyes wide. She gasped and giggled and paled at all the right moments, until John felt more confident and began to expand upon his tale.

He even told her about his longtime plans for Lady Bernadette and how she had come to visit Haven at his urging only to fall in love with Lord Matthias instead. From her expression, John gathered that Lady Emmeline believed her hostess must be verging on utter madness for making such an error. This was an added balm to John's recent decision to release his past yearnings. Lady Bernadette was all things favorable, but she was suddenly very clearly not the only possibility for Mr. John Barton, distinguished vicar of Haven.

At some point, John looked about him to realize that Lady Emmeline's relations had disappeared, including the abrasive Miss Grey. Only Miss Higgins remained as chaperone, dozing (complete with intentional snoring!) in the chair by the fire.

Somewhere in the house John heard a clock chime. When he pulled his watch from his waistcoat pocket, he was astonished to see that two hours had passed since he'd entered the lady's sickroom.

Lady Emmeline made a sweet pout at his departure, but she let him go without protest. From the little line forming between her brows, John guessed that her headache had worsened. He bowed himself out with a promise to check on her again tomorrow. Higgins walked him to the hall door.

"Milady left a message that you're to stay in the same room as you were. And that your things are all unpacked and that your mule is eating his lordship out of hay and oats at a rather fantastic pace and milord says don't you ever feed that blasted animal?" Miss Higgins gave John a conspiratorial wink and shut the door on him.

John sauntered thoughtfully back to his room, thinking of Lady Emmeline's astonishing eyes and her slender hand in his. He felt as though something very significant had just happened to him.

"At last. Haven't you any thought to poor Emmeline's condition? What are you thinking, keeping her up late after everything she's been through?"

John turned at his own door to see Miss Grey standing in her own doorway with her arms crossed over her bosom and her tawny hair down in a long braid that hung forward over one shoulder. She was, as usual, glaring at him. "Tell me, Vicar Barton, were you born so insensitive or have you been developing your gift for years?"

John's slight smile faded and his back stiffened. "I beg your pardon, Miss Grey, but Lady Emmeline asked me to stay and talk."

Miss Grey openly rolled her eyes at him. "Lady Emmeline is well trained to say whatever a gentleman might want her to say. If you'd wanted her to cry and flail herself into your arms, she would have discerned that as well and delivered accordingly!"

John stepped back, appalled at her view of her own entirely inoffensive cousin. "How can you openly accuse her of being so manipulative?"

The lady had the good grace to flinch from his anger. "I'm not accusing her of being manipulative. I'm accusing you of being susceptible to it. It unfortunately further convinces her that it is the only way she will ever be sought after." Miss Grey held up her hands. "As if you cared. Forget I said anything. Men are all the same, vicars included. You all want to hear it so badly, you'll take it any way you can get it." She narrowed her eyes at him, then stepped forward until she stood close enough for him to detect the meadow-flower scent of her.

"You're the most handsome man I've ever seen," she stated flatly, her voice practiced and mechanical. "I'm astonished at your incredible intelligence and devastated by your manly, manly muscles. Please, tell me every mundane detail about yourself because you are endlessly fascinating to me—and I'll pretend not to notice that you never, ever ask me a single thing about what I like or long for, or heaven knows, what I actually really think about anything."

John's gut twisted at the recognition that it was true. In the last two hours he'd not managed to ask Lady Emmeline anything about herself. Or if he had made a half-hearted effort, she'd waved her hand negligently and turned the conversation back to him. He'd allowed it, so eager had he been to impress her.

Then Miss Grey's words, scalding and judgmental as they were, made him smile. "My muscles are manly-manly? Is that better than simply being manly? Am I doubly manly because you said it twice?" When she only stood there, gaping at his unexpected reaction, he impulsively reached out to tug at her braid. "I'll take that as a yes," he whispered.

Her hair filled his hand, soft and warm in his palm. The braid was untidy, full of escaping wisps that twined around his fingertips. John released it slowly, his fingers exhibiting a strange reluctance to let go.

He bowed shortly. "Goodnight, Miss Grey. Do sleep well."

He shut the door on her standing there, her lips still parted in stunned surprise. He'd enjoyed having the last word, something for which he did not normally strive. It would be an unworthy occupation for a vicar, in his thinking. However, Miss Grey seemed a very worthy opponent indeed.

HIGGINS THE DRIVER was much like his sister, Higgins the lady's maid. Same button nose, same bright eyes. Burly instead of curvaceous, but other than their figures, they could swap their livery and exchange caps. It might take all day for anyone to notice.

This notion made Norah smile the next morning as she tapped on the door of the single men's servant quarters. It opened to reveal an astonished baby-faced under-footman.

"I have a tray for Mr. Higgins."

She did, a proper gentleman's breakfast of eggs and bacon. At the last moment, Cook had thrown on a small pitcher of milk and a few extra pats of butter for the rolls.

"It's good for broken bones," the arrogant cook had said gruffly. "Miss," he'd added with a dismissive nod.

The people in this house! The Grey family retainers were a loyal bunch but had grown casual in their service over the many underpaid years. They had all liked Norah because she did for herself and Emmeline without complaint. It was comfortable and occasionally exasperating but Norah was used to it.

The under-footman, who she doubted had yet required a razor, tried to take the tray from her. Norah held on grimly even as she smiled unrelentingly.

To her surprise, he finally took a hesitant step back and bowed her through the door no lady should even wish to knock upon.

Norah, quite frankly, was weary of everyone in the house and wanted an opportunity to talk to the man who had saved the lives of herself and Emmeline, the man she had helped, the one she'd befriended on the long cold trip from Kewell Abbey.

Baby Cheeks followed her as she bustled forward through the doorway. She heard him muttering something about "Mr. Jasper" and "skin me, he will!"

"Which room, please?" Norah's smile was fixed on "pleasant man management" as she tried very hard not to laugh at the youngster's quandary.

Clearly unable to refrain from answering a direct question from a lady, the fellow gulped and nodded at a door. "That one, Miss. But—"

Too late. Norah had expertly balanced her laden tray on one open palm and tapped on the door.

"Mr. Higgins? It's Miss Grey. Might I enter?"

At the startled affirmation from within, Norah swept into the small attic room like a lady in her own house. It worked every time.

Higgins was sitting up in bed, quite decently clad in a nightshirt and covered by a coverlet. His shoulder was strapped down tightly with his arm wrapped to his damaged ribs, the bandages showing just above the neck of the shirt.

"Oh, miss! I don't—I mean, it's right fine of you to visit, but—no, Brand, you stay!"

Norah smiled over her shoulder at Baby Face Brand. "Yes, do.

There's an iced bun in it for you if you'll play chaperone."

Young enough to be tempted by the treat and old enough to know the value of a chaperone, Brand took his bun and stood guard just outside the open door. It was a fine idea, for the ceiling slanted fiercely and even Norah had to bend a little.

She set up Mr. Higgins with his tray and poured tea for them both from the pot beneath its cozy. Mr. Higgins looked pained to eat before her, so Norah tore off a piece of a roll and popped it into her mouth. "Cook says the milk will do you good."

"Milk," Mr. Higgins scoffed. "Like I'm only knee-high!"

Norah raised an authoritative brow and pointed at the milk. Mr. Higgins, who was a good-natured fellow when not grumpy from pain and enforced bed rest, drank the "blasted milk."

Norah settled into the small room's only chair. She looked about the chamber with a frown. A driver for a wealthy house should have finer quarters than a coffin of a room he couldn't stand up in.

Mr. Higgins, who understood Norah quite well after days on the road, just chuckled. "Not to worry, miss. 'Tis handy to the door for nursing is all. His lordship has given me a fine room with a proper clothes press for my livery and all. I'll take it once I'm ready for duty."

Norah smiled at her friend. "Well, that's fine then. One less ornery male for me to bully into correct behavior."

Mr. Higgins nearly snorted his milk up his nose at the thought of Norah taking on Lord Matthias. Then he shrugged. "Might that you could, miss, being so fearless and all."

Norah shook her head. "Not fearless, Mr. Higgins. I simply don't give a fig what Lord Matthias thinks of me."

Eyes wide, Mr. Higgins nodded. "Fearless, miss, and don't you ever forget it. Do you think I don't recall you pulling me out from under that shattered nightmare of a carriage, miss? Thought the whole thing were going to fall on me head, I did. Saying me prayers, miss. Only regret I could come up with was ever leaving Haven in the first place."

Norah nodded politely. She was happy to change the subject. "I saw it as we drove through. It looks a charming village in truth."

Mr. Higgins's eyes crinkled. "'Tis pretty enough, but the north be full of pretty places." He shook his head. "No, Haven is special, miss."

"Surely most people think their home is special." Well, she didn't but she was merely an occupant of Kewell Abbey. It wasn't really her home.

Her home was something else. She had only ever seen it in her mind, recalled by a certain window here, a graceful hearth there. It would be a good house but not a "fine" one. She'd had her fill of gilded poverty, of fine useless things that had to be polished even when the larder was empty.

If it had been up to her, every gleaming bibelot in the Abbey would have been sold to pay wages, or to put something rather more useful than dahlias in the gardens, or make a proper order from the butcher.

In the end, Lady Emmeline's inheritance had saved them just in time—but Norah didn't believe such a heaven-sent gift was on its way to her.

She would never have the shining wholesome house she treasured in her most secret dreams, one full of laughing children and cheerful hearth fires—and that one person who would look up and smile every time she walked into the room.

"—horses, right miss?"

Norah blinked herself back to the wintry present. "So sorry, Mr. Higgins. I was off gathering wool. What was that?"

"Never knew there could be two such contrary horses in a pair, I said. One with all the brains, the other with not a one. Nothing but north wind blowing twixt the ears of that foolish lump of meat."

Norah smiled wryly. Mr. Higgins had amused her on the journey with his colorful descriptions of "that sorry beast," and his many flaws. Her favorite was when he'd pulled a big soft ear down to his own and listened theatrically. "Methinks I hear the sea."

"Lady Emmeline chose them," she reminded him now.

"Aye, they're a showy pair. Lady Emmeline knows fashion right enough, I'll wager. I just wish she would've taken me horse-trading with her."

Norah nodded, wishing she had done many things differently. She wished she had been kinder to the handsome, valiant stranger on the bridge. She wished she had talked some sense into Emmeline.

She wished she hadn't come along to Havensbeck at all, not if she'd only come to watch the only man she'd ever fancied fall under Emmeline's exquisite spell.

Norah lifted her chin and covered her regret with a smile. "So, Mr. Higgins, what is so special about Haven?"

"It's love, miss."

Surprised that a tough country fellow like Mr. Higgins would speak so openly about love, Norah straightened. "Ah. You left your girl behind?"

Mr. Higgins grinned. "Might be. I came home to find her, I did. Hope to meet her very soon. That's the wonder of it, don't you see, miss? People come to Haven and they step right into love, every time."

A brief sound of disbelief broke from Norah. Or perhaps it was belief, the tragic realization that someone she knew had done just that—except that the love John Barton had stepped into was Emmeline's, not hers.

Then sanity returned. "Vicar Barton has been here for nigh on two years now."

Mr. Higgins only looked triumphant. "Aye, but the vicar was already in love when he arrived, wasn't he?" He tapped his head. "It was me and my sister what figured it out. The vicar had his heart set, so the magic didn't work on him, did it?"

John's heart had been set on Lady Bernadette. Yes, of course. Now he was open to love again—just in time to catch pale, perfect Emmeline in his arms like an angel, a gift fallen straight from heaven.

A gift from Haven.

"So I'll be meeting my true love any time now. Or as soon as I get out of this blasted—beg your pardon, miss. Out of this fine bed his lordship has provided me while I heal."

Norah laughed. "Pray, don't strain yourself on my account, Mr. Higgins. There's not much worse than being bedridden." Unless one has a handsome heroic young vicar kneeling at one's bedside.

Thoroughly weary of herself, Norah stood, nearly knocking her head on the ceiling. "Perhaps I shall visit this magical wonder of the village then."

Mr. Higgins grinned and tugged on an imaginary cap. "You do that, miss. Go into the village. Magic, it is. Blessed. You'll see."

Chapter 7

B EFORE NORAH TOOK the lane to the village, she walked curiously about the grounds of Havensbeck.

There wasn't much to see under the thick, lovely blanket of snow. The world seemed to be asleep—or perhaps it simply waited, only dozing, ready to burst forth at the first hint of spring weather.

When she came into the cobbled stable-yard, swept clean of snow by the cheerful stable boys, Norah decided to check on the brave horse, the one with the brain. She gave the creature a pat and approved its spacious stall and gleaming coat.

An eager head thrust itself from the next stall and Norah found herself patting the velvety nose of the brainless horse. Against all odds, he seemed perfectly well and utterly unharmed, unlike his weary and still nervously twitching partner.

Norah sighed. What a gift it must be to be without thought or regret. Yesterday and the day before had utterly slipped away from this horse's thoughts. He nibbled at her fingers with soft lips and cast a longing, wistful look from his dark, liquid eye.

The silly thing thinks I owe him a sugar lump. "I believe I'm the one owed a treat, not you," she murmured, although she did scratch his empty forehead and smile at the notion of listening for the sea.

Then again, perhaps it was not an enviable thing, to live unconscious of consequences. To shy away from harmless little whirlwinds of snow, caught by the breeze over the river bridge. Poor silly beast.

"Some of us can't help but shy away from insubstantial things."

Like hope. Like love.

"All right, Mr. Higgins," she murmured. "Let us see this magical village of yours.

THERE WAS ONLY one way in and out of Havensbeck. Of course.

Yet Norah's gut chilled as she found herself upon the bridge, the scene of so much fear. Her feet stopped moving. She could go back. She didn't have to cross this scene of near tragedy.

However, now that Emmeline seemed to be recovering quickly, Norah decided to face that terror and all the regrets that came with it.

She walked along the deadly stone wall, her fingertips brushing at the few inches of fresh snow that had fallen. There was the place where she had climbed beneath the carriage to help Mr. Higgins. She could see the scrapes and streaks of lacquer on the stone wall where the carriage had dragged along it.

There, just beyond, was the site of her blackest nightmares. The careening carriage, its path swerving widely as the horses fought for control. The wheels skidding and the carriage sweeping sideways as she and Emmeline were tossed about within it.

Emmeline falling against the door. The door flying open at the impact. Norah's desperate grab for Emmeline's skirts as her cousin began to fall out.

And the stone wall that had seemed to rush at them as the carriage swung back around.

Emmeline, just beginning to gain her grip on the doorframe, mere seconds away from the moment Norah might have pulled her back to safety.

Norah heard again the way the fine lacquered carriage cracked like an egg against the unforgiving stone. The way Norah had been flung forward, hard on her knees.

She felt again the slip of silk sliding through her fingers. The sight of Emmeline falling backward, her frightened gazed fixed on Norah's.

Norah's hands fisted hard, once again grabbing tight.

Emmeline's hands splayed out, pale and weak against the evening sky, reaching for rescue that wasn't there.

Emmeline bouncing sickeningly off the wall and then slipping, sliding over it. Her weight dragging Norah forward until she braced her boots on either side of the cracked doorframe, her fists tightened beyond pain, and only sheer will keeping a grip on Emmeline who now dangled out of sight over the wall.

Norah hadn't dared move for fear the doorframe would give way, or her hands would, and her fingers were numb now and what if she lost her grip without realizing it and there was nothing left to do but scream—

"Shh. There is nothing to fear now."

A deep voice came, warm and calm and soothing. Gentle hands lifted her from her terrified crouch in the snow. Her vision still focused on terror in the past, she staggered. Strong arms closed about her, giving her a warm solid chest to shiver against.

Her hands, fisted so tightly—*don't let go!*—that her fingers ached. Her face was wet and freezing, tears feeling like crystals on her cheeks. The nightmare receded slowly, one sense at a time, until the wind across the snow replaced the screams of horses, the screams from her own throat.

Her gloved hands loosened, spreading across that solid chest by themselves, blindly seeking warmth and solidity. She gripped his coat, holding on as the careening world steadied, until her feet came back stand on the inevitable stone.

Norah's breath steadied. Not sobs but the open-mouthed panting of something hopelessly terrified.

"Y—you c—came."

John Barton rocked her gently as they stood there. "Yes, I'm here. You're here. Lady Emmeline and Miss Higgins are here as well, safe at the manor. Everyone will be as good as new, just like before."

Norah didn't explain that she'd meant that awful day, when she'd seen the silk slipping through fingers that felt nothing at all. She didn't tell him that by the time he called to her to release Emmeline, she already had. She shut her eyes tight against the vision of the hem of the silk dress sliding through her useless fingers, the flutter of it going over and out of sight—

"Hush. Be done. It is done. All is well, Norah." Warm fingers caught at her chin. He'd taken off his gloves to touch her, to lift her face from where it still pressed to his coat. "Look. The day is bright. Can't you feel the sun?"

She turned her head, eyes shut, seeking the touch of weak winter sun on her cheeks, the gleam of it beyond her closed eyelids.

Listen," he murmured. "So peaceful here today, so quiet. Even the river is silent today. Have you ever heard the like?"

Norah rested her cheek against his chest and listened. Naught but far distant sounds from the manor and the steady beat of John Barton's valiant heart beneath her ear, and the faint rustle of her skirts as he continued to sway with her in his arms.

No, I have never heard the like.

He is holding me. Me.

Close, so close. His clean masculine scent filled her every breath and she drank in his warmth, his strength and his kindness.

How I wish I were beautiful so I could make this man love me.

This man who looked at Emmeline with such fascination, who held her beautiful hand with such attentive care.

This strong, gentle, kind man who would be so good for Em, who would lend his steadiness and goodness to her flightiness and occasional self-centeredness.

The notion that Emmeline might not be so very good for John Barton tried to slide across Norah's mind, but lifelong habits of love and family loyalty swept it aside before it could gain purchase.

Two more breaths, a few more powerful heartbeats—those she stole for herself before she straightened and stepped back out of his embrace.

JOHN WASN'T SURPRISED when Norah—Miss Grey—stepped out of his arms. He'd felt her gathering the strength to stand on her own and had known her need for him was passed.

What did surprise him was that he had wanted her to stay right where she was. Prickly, suspicious Miss Norah Grey, held as carefully as a wild thing in his hands.

Brave, forthright Miss Norah Grey. Secretive, too, for had she not hidden her own lingering fear and trauma until she stood on this bridge and faced it down alone?

Miss Grey took another step back and turned away to tug her bunched skirts aright. After brushing quickly at her cheeks, she retied her fallen bonnet back over the tawny hair wound and pinned tightly to her head.

Her posture returned to her customary poker-straight invincibility but she took one more deep breath, letting it out slowly before she turned back to face him.

"Thank you, Vicar Barton," she said simply.

John liked that she'd not insulted him or herself with exclamations of embarrassment or regret or gushing appreciation.

After all, it took some doing to get normal civility from this woman. Such brief and sincere thanks from her meant more than hours of effusive gratitude from any dozen ladies.

"You're very welcome, Miss Grey." He bowed and then held out an elbow. "Shall we walk together into the village? I am due there very soon."

She hesitated. Then with a familiar touch of defiance, she lifted her chin. "I am quite able to walk down a country lane without assistance, sir." Yet she fell into step beside him.

John felt rather ludicrously as if he'd received an award. Miss Grey reminded him of a fox he befriended as a boy. The wild thing was never a pet, oh no. Yet John had felt honored by the way it came to tolerate his presence and sometimes even warily snatch a treat from his extended hand.

Striving to entice guarded Miss Norah Grey to tolerate me is clearly the desperate goal of a friendless man.

So why did he feel so cheerful as he stomped down a snowy lane with her at his side?

AS NORAH AND Vicar Barton marched along the lane together, Norah felt her spirits lifting with the cheeriness of the bright day.

Winters at Kewell Abbey were darker and colder somehow, or perhaps that had been because of the leaky old walls and the scarcity of coal for any but the main rooms. It wasn't poverty, or at least the elderly grandeur of the place didn't quite permit that word. It was simply long cold seasons of not-quite-enough.

That was all in the past now, due to Lady Emmeline's inheritance. No more chilled ankles or weak extended soups, or nights of Emmeline climbing into bed with her, Em's fashionable thinness having cost her the ability to keep warm.

Nothing, not even eating bread and watered soup all winter, could carve Norah down to such willowy elegance.

Thinking back to the bridge, Norah thanked the heavens the vital tug of war had not been reversed. She would have pulled Emmeline right over with her.

For Emmeline would never have let go.

Norah shivered.

Done. It was done, just as John Barton had said to her. She turned to look through her bonnet at the vicar.

"You have not cursed even once this morning, Vicar Barton. Are you feeling quite yourself?"

Why did such things come out of her mouth? At least, why did they come out the way they came out, so snappish and awkward? She could only hope he would take it well. She could not have been more surprised when he burst into laughter and then grinned ruefully at her.

"Tis true enough! You must think the worst of me, a man of the church with such a—a—"

"Picturesque vocabulary?"

He chuckled again, rubbing one palm over his face. "I am accurately skewered."

"Yet you seem... relieved somehow. Happier perhaps?" Happy to have met the beautiful Lady Emmeline? Happy to have fallen headlong in love with said lady, just as every man who ever encountered Emmeline seemed to do?

He shrugged at that and looked away. "'Relieved' is perhaps a good enough word. I have been relieved of my own tendency to clutch on too long."

"Ah." Norah nodded sagely. "Lady Bernadette."

John Barton whipped his head around to stare at her. "You've been here for only a few days! How could you possibly—" His expression fell. "Oh drat. Everyone must know what a fool I've been, if even you have discerned it so quickly."

Norah shrugged. She wasn't one to be patient with self-flagellation. It was, in her opinion, simply another symptom of being overly concerned with oneself. "I'm glad to hear that you've grown past it. Awkward, being sweet on your benefactor's wife. Must make for some deeply embarrassing moments."

"I was too busy wallowing to be embarrassed," he muttered, sticking his hands into his coat and walking with his head hanging.

Norah rolled her eyes, and she turned her head to be sure he saw it. "I meant 'embarrassing for her ladyship,' you mooncalf."

He stopped walking and just stared at her, his lips parted in astonishment. "The things you say." He shook his head and started to chuckle. "Mooncalf!"

He was laughing again. At himself, moreover, not at her.

Norah, who had always found her own company to be highly diverting, had never before met someone who agreed with her. His rich laugh at his own expense tugged an answering smile to her lips. Daft man.

He looked a little startled at her expression. Then his handsome face split in such a delighted grin that she blinked under the brilliance of it.

"Aha! I've caught you out!" he announced gleefully. "You have a lovely smile, Miss Grey." He leaned close to whisper conspiratorially. "I advise caution in its overuse. You wouldn't want everyone to know."

Then, having absolutely no notion of how he'd spun her very world around, he marched onward toward the village.

Norah followed automatically, her feet taking action while her mind was caught in a spinning maelstrom of disbelief.

You have a lovely smile.

Her. Miss Norah Grey, plain but useful poor relation.

Oh blast. How was she ever supposed to recover from something like that? Said by someone like him? Alone together in a snow-swept landscape yet, under a glittering winter sun?

It was one thing to admire someone in the privacy of one's own mind, someone far away and unattainable. That made it feel safe, like a riveting story that nevertheless, one might someday forget. It was quite another when that person looked at you—truly looked at you!—and liked what he saw.

I'm in such a pickle now.

Chapter 8

NORAH AND VICAR Barton walked into the village, which consisted of several cottages surrounding a square that might be a bustling place on a summer market day, but now lay peaceful beneath a covering of snow. Trails of bootprints crisscrossed the open square, leading from the inn to the milliner's, from the blacksmith's to the sweet shop.

Cheerful windows wore their holiday finery and a handwritten sign in the sweet shop read "Roasting chestnuts to-day!"

The few people passing bobbed their heads at John Barton and herself. "Vicar. Miss." They looked as if they knew her, and some turned to watch them pass.

"Miss Grey, I believe you are quite the sensation in Haven." Vicar Barton's murmur was amused.

Norah cast a wary eye on a man standing in the doorway of the inn. The short, stocky fellow smiled and nodded approvingly at her. "Whyever for?" she whispered.

"Oh, the Higgins family is very popular in Haven. They've been here for generations. You saved a Higgins, so you practically saved Haven itself." He shook his head. "It took me nearly a year to win over the Higgins family. Only by vastly overpaying Mrs. Higgins to care for the vicarage did I make any headway." He smiled. "Although she does a fearsomely fine job. I hardly dare drop a crumb in my kitchen."

Norah smiled to think of handsome young Vicar Barton having to prove himself to his own housekeeper. She cast him an arch glance. "Perhaps if you are very nice to me, I shall put in a good word with Mrs. Higgins."

He smiled back. "I'd very much appreciate it. Those crumbs, they do keep dropping." He stopped walking. "I'm afraid I must leave you here. Unless you'd like to come in?"

"Come in?" Norah realized that they stood before a very pretty church, set just on the far side of the square. "Goodness, how fine! And so large for such a small village!"

He nodded with quiet pride. "The village, the surrounding farms and all of Havensbeck's staff and tenant farmers too. And its lord and lady of course."

"Ah. Lord Matthias must be a good landlord. Everyone looks very prosperous."

"His lordship is a very good man, and Lady Bernadette is passionate about the village. Most of the local people are." He smiled. "There is a local legend, of sorts, that everyone who comes to Haven falls in love."

Norah's smile became a bit stiff but Vicar Barton didn't seem to notice. "Do tell?"

"I suppose that every village wants to have their own story," he replied. "But it is true that everyone in Haven is a dyed-in-the-wool romantic. They've been openly trying to wed me off for two years."

Norah looked out across the square so that her bonnet shielded her expression. "How terrible for you." She knew her voice dripped with irony but she couldn't help it. Never in her life had anyone lifted a finger to wed her off. The entire world assumed that no man would ever find her acceptable, and wasn't she lucky that her pretty cousin would surely marry well and take care of her forever?

The bell above them tolled the hour. Suddenly, the square became awash with running children, all of them storming toward the vicar and Norah like the hordes of Genghis Khan invading China.

"Eep." Norah didn't know anything about children and there really were so very many of them!

The vicar took her elbow in support and leaned close to speak into her ear. "Show no fear! They'll eat you alive!"

The flood of small persons parted around them where they stood. Little shoes and boots pounded up the steps of the church and burst the doors apart to flow inside. It was over in seconds. It had only seemed like hours.

"Now I really must go. If I leave them alone for too long, dire things happen."

She could imagine. "Go! Please!"

He bowed and ran lightly up the steps. As he opened one side of the double doors, he turned. "You are very welcome to watch, if you have time. We've been working very hard."

As Norah had nowhere else to be and she didn't much care for the idea of exploring a village that knew everything about her while she felt a stranger, she climbed the steps and preceded the vicar into the church.

There was no one there. Norah looked around but didn't see a single child. Then a wave of giggles rose somewhere over her head and she stepped forward to see the invading multitudes had taken position in the choir loft. Bright eyes and cheerful smudged faces peered down at her.

Norah had to smile in turn. They were so endearing, like fearless baby monkeys in a tree. One curly haired lassie wiggled her fingers at Norah. Norah waved to her.

Beside her, the vicar sighed. "And she wins over yet another Higgins."

"It's a children's choir! Oh, Emmeline would love to hear them!" Norah tried to think of some way to bring them together, but Vicar Barton beat her to it.

"She will hear them perform at the Christmas Eve Ball at the manor. 'Tis a new tradition." He stepped forward and clapped his hands. "Places, please!"

He was clearly an experienced director, for the little monkeys all hurried into more or less straight rows, tallest in the back. He pointed out a good seat for Norah and she took it, folding her hands in her lap and sitting forward eagerly.

First, the vicar took them through a series of rhyming exercises to warm up their voices. Then he had the different sections hum together to create a chord that surprised Norah with its power. Goodness, they were very well-schooled!

Then, with a wave of his hands, the vicar led his singers in a lovely Christmas carol. The piercing sweetness of the small voices flowed through the church like the scent of caramel on a stove. The vaulted ceiling and the delicate stone ribs supporting it seemed to ring the music back at them, augmenting and clarifying the sound.

"God rest ye, merry gentlemen
Let nothing you dismay..."

Norah could hardly pay attention to the familiar words, so swept away was she by the high lilting voices. Nothing could disrupt the sweet ache rising within her in response to the beauty of it, not the occasional lisp, or slightly sharp note, or the poor lad in the back who might not end the year with the same voice he'd began it.

Don't worry, Emmeline will have children.

Yes, and that would be lovely. Yet Norah was beginning to realize that her own contentment with that plan had been a canny bit of self-delusion. After all, why bother dream of something that would never happen?

Yet dream she did. Whole pieces of her felt fit to shatter at the hopelessness of that dream. Basic human instinct or maternal higher calling, it didn't matter. *I want a child. Actually, I want several, boys and girls of varying sizes—*

There was just one tiny hitch in the plan that bloomed joyfully in her soul at that moment.

"Which brings tidings of comfort and joy,
Comfort and joy..."

She was weeping again, for the second time today.

The song faltered. Norah dabbed at her eyes with her handkerchief and looked curiously up into the choral loft.

A little dark-haired boy had stepped out in front of the rest. All the other children were looking at him. Norah saw that even John Barton looked at the little fellow expectantly.

The boy was staring downward in terror.

At her.

Norah did her best to look harmless. She couldn't begin to think what about her could have inspired such alarm in the child.

The vicar cleared his throat. "Let's try that again from the chorus..."

The child hunched his shoulders and looked ashamed.

"...tidings of comfort and joy, comfort and joy!
Oh-oh, tidings of co-omfort and joy."

The next part should have been the verse of "In Bethlehem, in Israel" and Norah leaned forward, for it was her favorite part. She imagined the sweet voice of the little boy singing it out to fall upon the graceful church and a smile readied itself on her lips.

Instead, the child opened his mouth and uttered nothing at all.

The rest of the children began to giggle now. Norah ached a little. He could be no more than seven or eight years and it was clear that the moment of singing before a stranger was too much for him.

Mortified, the boy tried again. A painful squeak was all he managed before clapping his mouth shut and turning a deep red.

The monkeys in the loft erupted into actual laughter then. The little boy fled the loft.

The moment Norah heard his little boots pounding down the stairs, she made for the front door of the church. She was already standing outside braced for impact when he raced out onto the steps.

She caught him in her arms and swung him around to set him on his feet again. "Goodness, there's a runaway horse in the church!"

She chattered on matter-of-factly as the child, his explosive departure interrupted, seemed to fold in on himself.

"Now I suppose you'll tell me that you're in 'a terrible hurry and excuse me, miss' but I do believe that you ought to have a think first."

She sat him down on the top step and settled down beside him. There was no point in worrying about the state of her very ordinary gown or her nondescript gray cloak. Emmeline would never sit on a step, but Norah had no silks to ruin.

"I love that part of the song." Norah hummed for a moment. Then she sang lightly, "*In Bethlehem, in Israel,*

This blessed Babe was born
And laid within a manger
Upon this blessed morn."

On the inner side of the doorway, John halted and listened. Miss Norah Grey's singing voice was very fine, the ancient words lilting and poignant in her breathy soprano.

"*The which His Mother Mary*
Did nothing take in scorn."

Miss Grey let the melody trail off and sighed. "It's one of those songs that is both happy and a little sad, isn't it? Christmas is like that, too. We are happy because we feast and celebrate and give gifts. We are sad because someone good and fine is gone now."

Sniffle. "Jesus."

"Oh yes, Jesus... and other people. People that I miss. Is there someone you miss at Christmas time?"

Inside the church, John could've kicked himself. He'd known perfectly well that little Arthur's grandmother had passed on last spring. He'd presided over the funeral, for pity sake! Now that he bothered to have a thought outside his own situation, he recalled that the elder Mrs. Tanner's greatest joy had been Arthur's fine voice and his role as soloist in the choir.

"My Nan, Miss. It doesn't seem right singin' on Christmas without her."

"Yes, I know what you mean. My father loved to play chess with me. After he passed away, I couldn't even touch the game without wanting to cry."

John leaned to one side to see Miss Grey take skinny Artie Tanner under one arm, tucking him against her side.

"You've left your coat inside, you know," she told him. "You'd best fetch it before you go home." Her tone was gentle but matter-of-fact. "What would your Nan say if you walked home without your coat?"

Little Artie sniffled. "She'd have said I'd no more sense than a day-old chick." He rubbed his sleeve over his eyes. "And she'd flick my ear but good, she would." He rubbed his un-flicked ear woefully.

"And what would she say if she knew you'd left your choir practice?"

"She'd have given me a biscuit for the hurt feelings and then she'd have made me scrub the pots for running out on a promise. And she'd have marched me back to say me regrets to the vicar."

John felt as though he ought to step in now, summoned as it were. Yet he was fascinated by Miss Grey's actions and he really wouldn't mind seeing if she had some sort of solution for little Artie.

"But you've sung your part in rehearsal before. Why didn't you want to sing it for me?"

"'Twasn't you, miss. Seeing you there, I thought about the manor and how everybody was goin' to be there..."

"Everyone but your Nan."

"Yes, miss." He scrubbed at his face again.

"What is your name?"

"Artie. Arthur Tanner, miss."

"Mr. Tanner, I am Miss Norah Grey. I'm a guest of Lord Matthias at Havensbeck Manor."

"Oh yes, miss. I know. Everybody knows you. Mrs. Higgins told my auntie, who told my mum, who told my da over dinner last night.

You save people."

John smiled behind his concealing door. The Legendary Miss Grey.

He heard a squeal and a protest coming from the choral loft above his head. He'd have to fetch Artie back inside and get back on task or something was going to go very awry upstairs.

John took one step closer to the door.

"That's right, I do save people. Shall I save you too?"

What? John enjoyed Miss Grey's flights of originality, but he didn't want her to mislead a young boy.

"Yes, miss. Only could you save my mum instead?"

"Why does your mum need saving?"

"She's too upset. She was so tired from the new babe that she missed Stir-Up Sunday!"

"Oh dear. That's a shame."

It certainly was. John knew that Stir-Up Sunday, the last Sunday before the beginning of Advent, was the day in which every cook in England put their Christmas pudding in the sack to age. It would be far too late for Mrs. Tanner to begin now, only days from Christmas, which meant there would be no figgy pudding, that heavy, chewy cake stuffed with dried fruit and candied peel, at the Tanner house.

"She meant to do it. But it was Nan who always made it and my mum didn't recollect to get all the ingree—ingrid—"

"Ingredients, yes." Miss Grey sighed. "The recipe calls for a great many."

"So if I could, miss, I'd like to give my saving to my mum."

"Hmm. I suppose... if you can complete the heroic quests, that is."

"Quests, miss? Like, slayin' dragons and such?"

"Oh, nothing so easy as that. You must complete three quests. It's traditional."

John bit back a laugh. She was mad, completely mad. He pressed closer to the door, unwilling to miss a word.

"Yes, miss!"

"Very well. Firstly, you must go inside and apologize to the vicar and your fellow singers. Soloist is a position of great responsibility, you know. It's like...like bearing the standard for the entire army! If the standard bearer goes down, the flag goes down and the battle is lost. You wouldn't want that to happen at the performance, would you?"

"No, miss!"

John could tell that little Artie was much impressed with his responsibility now.

"Secondly, you must help your mother at home. From now until the New Year, you must do one of your mother's chores so that she can rest. No one else can bear children but a mother, but anyone can put a hand to washing the dishes. Soldiers wash dishes, after all."

"They do?"

"Of course! A soldier doesn't take his mother with him to battle, does he?"

Miss Grey was going to have little Arthur Tanner enlisting at any moment. There was a thud and then giddy laughter from above. John dithered. He should get back to work but...

I want to know the third condition.

He told himself he was looking out for little Artie, but he knew he was simply outrageously curious what the ingenious Miss Grey would say next.

"Alright, miss. I'll do the dishes every day. What else I got to do?"

"Thirdly, you will sing your very best at the performance, because you are not singing at Christmastime without your Nan. She will be watching from Heaven, you know."

"Oh." Then, in a tiny awestruck voice, "With Jesus?"

"I should think so, yes," Miss Grey replied calmly. "It is his birthday, after all."

John managed to scramble several steps back from the door before he laughed.

Chapter 9

AFTER THRUSTING LITTLE Arthur Tanner back inside, Norah had waved away Vicar Barton's invitation to come back into the church. She'd done enough to disrupt what was likely one of the last rehearsals before the performance.

She only wished she knew why the vicar had smiled so warmly at her when she departed.

You have a lovely smile.

Ruthlessly, Norah tore that thought away and stomped across the square to the inn. She had a mission now.

At first she had simply assumed that she could purchase a figgy pudding somewhere, but this wasn't London or even Leeds. However, inns had cooks, so it seemed a good place to start.

After consulting the stout, smiling man, who turned out to be the innkeeper, Mr. Cranston, and who beamed painfully at her the entire time, he in turn brought out his wife. She bustled out from the kitchens, drying her hands on a towel and looking as busy as every homemaker must be just days before a celebration.

I, who have no home to make, am not busy.

Mrs. Cranston looked much less irritated after her husband introduced Norah properly. "Oh my, miss! How can I help you, Miss Grey?"

When Norah told the story of promising to help the Tanners with their Christmas pudding deficit, Mrs. Cranston looked rather desperately as if she wanted to cry.

"Oh poor Mrs. Tanner. She's such a young thing, too. She must be in a tizzy for sure. And I never knew. Old Mrs. Tanner made the best figgy pudding in the county and it would have been a tall order to live up to, even if she hadn't missed Stir-Up Sunday."

"I thought perhaps, being an inn, that you might have a spare pudding I could purchase for the Tanners?" Norah wasn't an heiress, but she had a few shillings of her own and little else to spend them on.

"Oh, aye. I made up a dozen. All gone up to t'hall, Miss Grey. Lady Bernadette arranged it. Paid me too much, but that's her way, to keep the custom in the village instead of sending away for fancy London goods. And there's no point to having that foreign manor cook have a go at a good Staffordshire figgy pudding!"

The "foreign" cook was from London, Norah happened to know.

Mrs. Cranston wrung her hands in her apron. "And it was Mrs. Tanner's recipe and all! Oh, I tried for ages to cajole that woman into sharing it—and she only did it this year when she knew she was close to passing. I should've thought it out on my own, miss. I'm that crushed that I didn't."

Norah was disappointed that it wouldn't be so simple. She surely didn't have enough coin to impress a prominent cook, who likely wouldn't sell one of milady's puddings anyway. Still, she had a secret weapon, didn't she?

No one ever refused Lady Emmeline anything.

"OH, HELLO VICAR!"

Swathed in knitted wool, red-cheeked and cheerful in defiance of the cold, Mr. Cranston stood guard at the door to his inn, the better to guide newcomers within to spend their coin.

When the children had settled down and given a single good rendition of their repertoire, John had released them. They were ready, even little Artie, who had stepped up and sung his piece with gusto. More rehearsal would only exhaust them and cause John frustration. One lad was in the thick of masculine voice change and two others trembled on the brink of it. Tiny Ruthie Higgins couldn't actually pronounce "Chrithmath."

Or "Jethuth."

Perfection was not the point. Joyous celebration was the object, and the little beasts certainly had their joy down pat.

So John, duty done and seeing the path set down in the snow by a decisive pair of lady's boots heading from the church steps toward the inn, had ambled over to see if Miss Grey would like to walk back to Havensbeck with him.

"Good day, Mr. Cranston. Is Miss Grey about?"

Mr. Cranston nodded sadly. "Oh aye. Poor thing."

John might have several opinions on prickly, tart-tongued, clever Miss Norah Grey, but "poor thing" had never crossed his thoughts.

"Oh? How so?"

Mr. Cranston sighed. "It's the village, you know. It can't be helped."

John frowned at the man. "I'm afraid I don't understand. Why is Miss Grey to be pitied?"

Mr. Cranston peered at John with something that might be curiosity. He took a breath, a serious one, as if he might be about to lay some particular enlightenment upon John. Then he shook his head. "Oh no reason, Vicar. Only her being disappointed about the pudding is all."

John had scarcely had the story from Cranston, regarding Miss Grey's quest to repair the puddingless Tanner family, before Miss Grey herself emerged from the inn. She had a tiny line between her brows that went away as she saw him. Her eyes went bright and somehow more green and a smile tugged at the corners of her mouth but didn't quite emerge.

Quite correct. Don't let the rest of the world see that smile.

It's mine.

Which was a very strange thought. Then again, it had been a strange day, hadn't it?

John stuck out an exaggerated elbow. "Your carriage awaits, milady."

She raised a brow. "We are on foot, Vicar Barton."

"'Tis a snow carriage, Miss Grey." *I think there might be something wrong with me.*

She smirked. "With invisible ice horses, I assume?"

John bowed. "And wheels made of giant snowflakes. But we mustn't tarry. 'Tis a slow-moving vehicle."

She snorted. "Hardly faster than a man can walk, I hear."

He straightened and smiled into her eyes. She was, once past all the sniping and snarling, a most amusing companion.

As they strolled away, John heard Mr. Cranston muttering.

"Poor little thing."

WHEN NORAH AND Vicar Barton reentered Havensbeck Manor, Norah was laughing at the vicar's tale of little Ruthie Higgins taking revenge on two of the boys who teased her about her lisp. Ruthie had set her biscuits from her lunch down and turned her back on them. When the two lads began to howl and run for the pump by the watering trough outside, they didn't dare tell John how they'd come to be eating someone else's lunch. Ruthie had batted her big eyes in astonishment and never said a word about how she'd sandwiched a thick layer of black pepper between the sweet biscuits, sealed with a bit of butter.

"It was Mrs. Higgins who told me the tale. I would have pointed out that she was boasting about her granddaughter's mischief to the wrong party, but I didn't want pepper in my biscuits!"

Norah was still grinning as they left their coats with two footmen in the foyer and entered the main hall.

Norah had intended to dash upstairs and change out of her boots and her gown with its wet hem, but then she stopped at the sight of the entire household gathered there. It was chaos, or at least a rather chaotic order. Everyone was involved in hanging ridiculous amounts of greenery and shimmering bits and bobs from anything that might hold them.

Even the chandelier was heavily festooned! Norah frowned up at it and wondered if she ought to mention the historically adversarial relationship of pine resin and flame.

"Don't fret, Nottie! Lord Matthias made it quite safe."

"Emmeline?" Norah peered past a trio of chambermaids who were rolling out simply miles of cheerful red ribbon to see that it was Emmeline indeed.

Her cousin sat in the center of the hall upon an upholstered chair with her feet up on an embroidered stool. So enthroned, she was absolutely swathed in throws and furs. She looked radiant and happy and very much better.

Norah put off changing to check on Em.

"Oh Nottie, don't fuss! Jasper is an absolute darling and I am resting, I really am. I was so bored up in that room by myself!"

Norah was fairly certain Emmeline hadn't been alone for even a single second since arriving at Havensbeck, but she couldn't deny the claim of boredom. She herself would be driven most righteously barmy after days in one room.

Norah felt John Barton at her side. He gave off a warmth. It felt like knowing when one has come close to the hearth. However, when she turned to smile at him, he seemed entirely fixed upon Emmeline.

As for Emmeline, she immediately went from bubbly and eager to wan and brave as she smiled tremulously up at him.

Resentment roiled within Norah. As always it was a mixed emotion, for she was as resentful that Emmeline was never allowed to be her own sweet, silly self around men as she was that Emmeline had so effortlessly entranced John Barton.

"Well," Norah said stiffly, "don't get Mr. Jasper in trouble with her ladyship by overdoing yourself." With that she turned on her heel and marched away from the both of them.

Back in her chamber, she changed quickly into dry things and if she spent a bit longer on her hair than usual, it was only out of respect for her hosts.

It certainly wasn't for the benefit of John Barton. She could spend a year before her mirror and not a moment of it would do her any good standing next to Emmeline.

As the forever battle of devil and angel, envy and love, wrestled on within her, Norah made herself return to the hall. She refused to deny herself an entertaining afternoon simply because Vicar John Barton forgot she existed on a regular basis.

It wasn't even his fault that he was blinded. Every male in the hall seemed to orbit around Emmeline's glamorous planet. Bees to a flower. With one exception.

Lord Matthias appeared to find Emmeline quite agreeable but it was in Lady Bernadette's glow that he basked. The poor man looked somehow both starved and self-satisfied at the same moment whenever his wife smiled brightly at him.

How does she do it? And does she give lessons?

"Oh Miss Grey!" The Havensbeck butler bustled up to Norah. "I wonder if you might assist young Brand and Tanner in hanging the garland on the stair? They mean well but they simply don't have an ounce of good taste between them. It looks like they're putting up a fence!"

Norah blinked. "And I have an ounce of good taste?"

Jasper smiled admiringly at her. "Of course, miss! You are always very nicely turned out. I do admire such elegant restraint in a lady."

He peered at her closely. "Although it is amusing to overdo once in a while, don't you find?"

Norah smiled up at the ridiculous joyous holiday display on assembly all about her. "Like at Christmas?"

Jasper nodded. "Lord Matthias does love a nice garland."

Or a clear hundred of them. Norah grinned at her two new partners in excess. "Hello again, Mr. Brand. And Mr. Tanner. Any relation to a charming young man by the name of Arthur?"

Tanner nodded earnestly. "My nephew, miss. His da is me eldest brother."

"Oh dear." Norah put a gentle hand on the young footman's arm. "My condolences on the loss of your mother this year. I know this is your first Christmas without her."

Mr. Tanner was a well grown fellow of twenty years or more, but his wide brown eyes filled at her words. "Thank you, miss. It's terrible kind of you to be concerned. We are all a bit low, but Artie was Nan's special pet and he's taking it very hard."

From across the room, John watched from his place at Lady Emmeline's side as Miss Grey spun yet another prominent Haven family into her web of kindness.

He shook his head. "And she's only been here a few days!"

Lady Emmeline followed his gaze. "Oh yes. Norah is always one to befriend the staff. At Kewell Abbey they all adore her."

John frowned at Lady Emmeline's not-quite-dismissive tone. "And how do *you* get on with the Abbey staff, Lady Emmeline?"

She twinkled adorably at him. "Oh, they like me just fine, especially since I made Papa pay all their back wages after I inherited."

John smiled and relaxed. She was a lady-with-a-capital L, as Simon would say. Of course she wouldn't have as easy a time crossing the boundaries of class and status as someone like Miss Grey. It was very honorable of her to see the debts paid to the servants, something John wished more of the nobility would manage responsibly. Not every master was as fair and generous as Matthias.

John waited for his inevitable feeling of betrayal at the thought of Matthias and was pleased and gratified to feel no such thing. All he felt for Matthias was goodwill and admiration and also a comfortable faith that Matthias would keep yesterday's confidence to his grave.

Suddenly restless with a sort of bubbling energy, he turned to Lady Emmeline. "Shall I find you a cup of tea? Perhaps a few of Cook's famous chocolate confections? He trained with a displaced French chocolatier, you know."

Lady Emmeline's expression became carefully polite. "Tea would be lovely, but I don't care for sweets." Then she looked across the hall where Miss Grey was now ordering Brand and Tanner about like her personal Christmas army. "Norah is quite partial to them, though. I'm sure she would enjoy them very much."

John rose and bowed. "Then I shall serve you both."

He was about to rush off when a dainty hand landed on his arm with a surprisingly firm grip. "Best bring Norah extra. Double." She sighed and wilted back upon her cushions, looking absolutely stunning and pitiful at the same moment.

John walked away thinking it was an odd sort of request. Had it come from someone less sweet-natured, he might almost have thought it a feminine slight, a catty reference to Miss Grey's more rounded figure.

John himself didn't mind a generous shape on a lady. It seemed very warm and womanly to him. His wayward male brain reminded him of the quite satisfying impact of Miss Grey's lush form on his own that morning in the hall.

Also, her smooth cheeks dimpled quite appealingly when she smiled. He enjoyed it so much he'd set out to amuse her with silly stories of village life on their walk back, just to wrest more smiles and earn that husky gurgling laugh.

The famous Havensbeck cook, hired by Lady Marianna herself, stood like a general on a battlefield in one of the manor's three vast kitchens. Around him, his minions chopped, steamed, braised and did all manner of activities about which John knew very little.

"Ahem."

Actually, the admirable fellow was rather polite about John's clearly strange request. John realized a little too late that in a great house like Havensbeck, one didn't simply leapfrog over the chain of command to speak to the cook.

Yet he walked away unscathed, followed by a liveried footman toting a tray holding a delicate tea service, a plate of tiny eggy pastries—"for Lady Marianna's cousin, who needs to regain her strength"—and a selection of screamingly elegant chocolates set in a probably priceless jeweled silver box.

I suppose I should've simply asked Jasper. It had been a very long time since John had lived in a house with a full staff—and they'd never actually been *his* staff, had they?

Chapter 10

SOON NORAH BEGAN to enjoy herself in earnest. Brand and Tanner were peas in a pod, both young enough to turn nearly everything into a game. Norah challenged them to a decorating race and divided the grand curving stair railing into three.

She showed them what she wanted and then climbed onto a ladder to reach her portion. "Ready. Steady. Go!"

There was a trick to winding the garland so that the twine stringing it together didn't show and Norah had more practice with it than the lads. When she saw she was winning, she hooted at them, reminding them of all the teasing they'd receive from the rest of the staff.

She needed to move the ladder. She knew she ought to, but she was so close and if she stopped now the young men with their longer arms would win. If she held on tight with one hand and just reached—

Too far. She realized the moment when the ladder began to tilt beneath her. In a panic she grabbed for the uprights of the stair rail but her fists only closed on balsam needles and twine.

"Norah!"

JOHN CROSSED THE room, smiling at the garland race. Several of the maids had stopped to watch and were cheering Norah onward.

"C'mon, miss! You've got 'em half frighted now, y'do!"

John slowed, balancing his tray. After Lady Emmeline had been served, John had snapped up the beautiful box of sweets to take to Norah, no footman required. He was going to make her laugh, bowing with his best butlery form, one arm crossed behind his back. She would play along and call him "Barton" and thank him with languid aristocratic indifference.

She was laughing now, twining her garland around the upright balusters with swift, sure movements. Her eyes were bright and her dimples were showing and her bottom was nicely outlined by her gown when she reached—

The ladder looked wrong. All wrong. *Please, God!*

His tray went spinning off to the side as he raced forward. "*Norah!*"

John didn't so much as catch her as he broke her fall, being that he was physically between her and the hard marble of the hall floor. She fell into him and he fell back into a press of bodies that gave way behind him. He heard gasps and shrieks and then he and Miss Grey both sprawled hard and awkwardly onto the floor.

Amid the cries from the others and the way the wind had been knocked right out of his lungs, it was all John could do to clutch at Norah, trying to keep her head from impacting the floor.

For a very long moment as his chest ached for lack of air and her wide eyes stared into his, John could not bear the fear that still filled him. Norah injured. Norah broken like a doll on the marble.

Norah gone.

John realized that he was lying on his back on the floor with a lady splayed on top of him and he was desperately clutching ... her bottom.

Then she was shoving at him, pushing herself up and away from him. John became aware that they had caused a ripple effect. Footmen and maids and guests were sprawled in a large area around them, inspiring images of concentric circles of collision, rippling outward.

Many hands reached to aid Norah to her feet and he could tell by the hot, painful flush on her face that she could scarcely bear not to knock away their hands.

He'd done a clumsy job of it, that was true, but he had certainly saved her from some serious injury and possibly death.

Norah gone.

He certainly hadn't been aiming for her bottom—soft and squeezable as it may be!

Pardon me, God.

I hope I don't get an erection. Oh damn, don't think about erections!

He scrambled up off the floor with the aid of a footman or three. Good Lord, his back hurt! Straightening with effort, he gently put aside the hands that tried to brush the fallen needles from his suit. "I'm perfectly fine, yes, thank you, no, all is well with me—"

Actually, he was a mess and there was something sticky down the back of his surcoat.

The hall was a muddle, too. Spilled trays and shattered glass ornaments and fallen greenery lay within the impact area, looking like an inexplicable Christmastide battlefield. *Well, that is simply appalling.*

Norah cast one humiliated, furious look his way. Her very posture said she'd like nothing better than to disappear. "Why are you so upset?" He moved closer. "Were you so very frightened?"

She jerked back from him.

Would it help to make a joke? Persuade her to laugh off the matter?

"I suppose I could have done that a bit more gracefully," he said to her with a self-deprecating shrug. *Ow.*

She flinched. "Yes, you could have. I've seen you do it, if you recall."

Ah yes, his rather stylish mid-air catch of Lady Emmeline. He'd had much more time to prepare that time, and she seemed to have forgotten that on that occasion he'd also landed on his arse. Or perhaps that bit hadn't been visible from her position in the carriage?

How could he explain that it was the fact that he might lose her which had stolen all sense and logic from his mind? How could he think about angles and velocity when he'd been blinded by visions of her shattered at his feet?

"Ah, perhaps this time I merely had stage fright before so many witnesses."

Her eyes flashed wild anguish at the thought of so many witnesses—or victims? Definitely the wrong tack to take. She looked around at the devastation and her complexion became blotchy with mortification.

"Or perhaps I am simply not beautiful enough to inspire your inner hero." Her voice was a familiar snarl but her eyes were filled with an extraordinary misery that he could not understand.

I offended her? I don't understand.

Then her words sank in and he could only stare, stunned by her unjust charge.

Lady Bernadette and Miss Higgins the maid were there now, urging Miss Grey to come along so they could check her over for injuries. He started to follow, but Jasper and Matthias were there, dragging him away for the same reason.

"I'm confused," he confessed to Matthias. "I saved her from a terrible fall. You saw that part, didn't you? Yet she seems to dislike me more than ever."

Matthias shook his head. "John, you're a bit of an idiot when it comes to women."

"I am not!" He glanced at Jasper, who only made a regretful face. "Am I? I *am?*"

Matthias guided him around a lake of spilled mulled wine being soaked up by rafts of deviled ham sandwiches. "John, women definitely prefer to be caught when they fall. They do not, as a rule, enjoy appearing like a breaching whale swamping a fishing boat. It violates some sort of directive of delicacy, I believe."

Jasper sighed. "Too right, milord. Ladies do dislike calling attention to their own physical existence." He peered at John, then shook his head. "Ladies don't like it when they're made to look fat."

Fat? Norah? John supposed she was a bit more well-formed than some ladies. His body was still trying not to react to the feeling of double handfuls of rich, soft bottom in his hands. And her bosom had squished very nicely against his chest as she lay upon him on the floor. But fat? Impossible. Norah wasn't fat, she was just … just Norah. "That is the daftest thing I've ever heard. You two just made that up."

Before they had taken more then a few more steps, Lady Emmeline appeared. Her tear-streaked face only seemed to set off those limpid violet pools she called eyes. Her pallor made her look as if her perfect features were carved of alabaster and the tiny crinkle between her brows turned her beauty tragic.

She flung both arms around his neck and pulled his head down to kiss his cheek. *Oh my flaming back.*

"Thank you, dear John, dear wonderful John! You saved my dear Norah! Oh, thank you!" She came in for another grab. John flinched.

Matthias must have felt it, for he gently detached Lady Emmeline and physically turned her around. "Your cousin needs you now, Lady Emmeline. Go to her." He even gave her a masterful little push that sent her trotting gracefully away, trailing her costly fur wrap on the spattered floor.

John gasped aloud at the continuing twinges shooting up his back. "Matthias, I take back every terrible thing I've ever thought about you. And the million times I almost hated you."

Matthias grunted as he slung John's arm over his shoulder. "That many?"

Jasper carefully took John's other arm on his shoulder. "Hot bath and a whiskey, Vicar Barton? Two whiskeys perhaps?"

"You are the world's most amazing butler, Jasper. There should be a gold cup for winning such a prize." He turned to Matthias, giddy in his gasping attempts to push aside the pain shooting down his legs. "Jasper needs a gold cup, my lord. Right away."

"It will be in his stocking when he wakes up on Christmas morn. Now, John the Valiant Vicar, shut it and walk."

NORAH ONLY JUST made it to her chamber before bursting into silly useless tears. Lady Bernadette seemed to think she needed a whiskey. Miss Higgins headed out to call for a nice hot bath.

Alone for a moment, Norah fought to pull herself together. What was wrong with her?

I am furious with him. With myself. With my life. With my face and my figure and my stupid tendency to say the oddest things.

He liked that about her, though. At least he seemed to.

Oh, she had been silly, hadn't she? Replaying that masterful catch off the frozen bridge in her mind, dreaming of such a romantic moment for herself someday. Emmeline had experienced that romantic moment and she didn't even remember it.

Well, Norah wasn't ever going to be able to forget hers. Oh, what a hideous mess!

Now Norah was shaking and the tears were still coming and she thought she might like to vomit every time she remembered the terrible moment when she overbalanced and realized with a sickening awareness that she'd climbed too high on the ladder and the fall was going to be very, very bad—

And then he came.

Lady Bernadette arrived with the whiskey and by the force of sheer lady-of-the-manor will persuaded Norah to drink it. It was awful. Then warmth and a sort of lightheaded relaxation began to ooze through her body. Her tears slowed and then stopped entirely.

"That's better." Lady Bernadette was kind but matter-of-fact. "Now, I certainly understand being frightened. That was a very close call. You could have been seriously injured."

With the distance of half an hour and a gulp or four of whiskey, Norah could nod calmly at that without starting up again with trembling and tears. She took another sip.

"I think I'd better take that now. Your mother might not approve."

Norah was herself enough to slide a wry look at Lady Bernadette. "You know, I'm fairly certain that I'm older than you are."

Lady Bernadette shrugged. "Only by a year. And I'm wed to a man who indulges me entirely, so I win. No, really. I win every single time."

She set the glass aside and turned to gaze at Norah with her arms folded. "Now, I'd like you to explain your rather rude attack on John Barton. You recall him? The man who raced across the room to fling himself bodily between you and simply miles of dangerously hard marble?"

He had?

"He must have been watching you quite closely. None of us had the slightest idea you were in trouble until he shouted your name. Then it was all falling pine needles and crashing ladders and most of the occupants of Havensbeck hitting the floor."

Norah felt just awful. "Oh the beautiful garland!" Then she hiccupped. She blinked hard. "I feel a bit odd."

"Well, you would feel odd, seeing that you're almost drunk." Lady Bernadette sighed. "My fault. I usually pour for Matthias and he's had a bit more practice than you have."

"Oh. That explains a great deal." Norah rubbed at her tingling face. "I fell on him. I squashed him flat, like stepping on a bug. The entire room falling down, because I'm too—too—" The memory hurt so. It was yet another sign that she was no man's lovely heroine. She looked up at Lady Bernadette and sniffled. "I'm too round. Too stout. Not like Em. He caught Emmeline like you might catch a falling leaf."

"Well, that's just nonsense," Lady Bernadette scoffed. "He wrenched his back and bruised his arse catching Lady Emmeline. He went to bed that night walking like a hundred-year-old man."

Norah blinked. "He didn't say anything to me."

Lady Bernadette crinkled her brow. "Whyever would he? And John didn't tell me, the doctor did."

No wonder John had been so cool to her at first. Goodness, she must have seemed so ungrateful to him! Oh, she wished she could go back.

"It's me," she whispered in a wash of wobbly shame. "I'm despicable when I'm frightened. I just snarl and snap!" She looked at kind, lovely, lucky Lady Bernadette. "It's panic. And then I can't bear for anyone to see me be so weak—" The sobs threatened to return, the nasty snotty maudlin sort. There might be wailing in her future as well.

Oh yes. Definitely wailing.

"Hm." Lady Bernadette's voice sounded resigned through Norah's yowls. "Higgins, if we put her in the bath right now, she's likely to drown. Leave it until we get some tea into her and for pity's sake, *don't* tell her family I gave her a man-sized glass of whiskey!"

Chapter 11

EMMELINE ENTERED NORAH'S bedchamber in a swirl of expensive scent and mink and cousinly concern. She wrapped her arms around Norah and held her tight. "Oh don't cry, Nottie! I'm here! Everything is all right now. I'm here."

She petted Norah soothingly and squeezed too tightly. The odd thing was, everything *was* better with Emmeline there. Money and men might come and go, but Emmeline would always and forever be on Norah's side in any battle or adversity. She was loyal and silly and charmingly oblivious to the end.

"I'm so embarrassed, Em," Norah wailed. "I squashed him! Everyone! Squash! Like a beetle, right on the floor!"

"Nonsense. You floated down like a rose petal. Your gown fluttered. Your hair still looks very nice, even after such an ordeal."

"Really?" Norah sniffed and patted her hair. "I think I'm drunk."

Emmeline blithely ignored the unladylike reference to drinking. "Oh yes. Did you use extra pins today?"

Norah blew her nose on her handkerchief, distracted from her wailing. "I did, actually."

"I told you so." Emmeline tucked Norah close and rocked her gently. "Now about that ladder. You're not allowed to die, Nottie. I won't have it."

Norah rested her head on Em's delicate shoulder, though it was a bit pointy.

Miss Higgins handed Norah a beautiful silver box. "This is for you, Miss. The vicar dropped it when you fell."

Norah blinked at the opulent gift. "From the vicar? For me? That can't be right."

Emmeline squealed. "It was saved! How divine!" She opened it to display the contents. "From me, too. I told him you'd like them. Lots of them!"

Norah gazed down at the bounty of expensive chocolates and

sighed. She wasn't opposed to a sweet now and then, but the world was under the impression that Miss Norah Grey ate them by the shovelful. It was Emmeline's doing. Her family role as sacrificial bride didn't allow her to indulge in anything that might ruin her figure, so for years Norah had been the one who took extra servings of sweets and then secretly shared them with Emmeline.

No one cared what Norah's figure looked like, after all.

The fact that John Barton now thought Norah devoured double servings of chocolates shouldn't bother her. What difference did it make?

Still, it stung.

Emmeline was working her way through the dainty treats, taking a single bite out of each one and sighing with childish delight. Of course, she was adorable. Norah couldn't stay angry with Emmeline. She never could.

The whiskey seemed to be wearing off a bit. The room wasn't spinning and Norah no longer felt the urge to wail. Miss Higgins's strong tea was bracing in itself. Norah rather thought it also might be very good for cleaning axle grease.

She looked up over her teacup rim to see Lady Bernadette studying both her and Emmeline with an expression of enlightenment on her usually cheerful features. Norah lowered her cup. "Yes, my lady?"

Lady Bernadette smiled slowly. "Neither of you are who you appear to be, are you?"

Norah felt defensive on Emmeline's behalf. "She has to behave that way. It's not her fault."

Emmeline twined her fingers with Norah's. "And Nottie helps me. I'd never be able to win the game without her."

"The game? Do you mean finding a husband?"

Emmeline gave a tinkling laugh that sounded like angels playing golden harp-strings. "Oh yes. That, too. The Society Game. The dance of status and social and political benefit." Suddenly Emmeline sounded like a cagey politician, which wasn't surprising considering Uncle Bester's behind-the-scenes involvement in Parliament.

Norah nodded. "It's a blood sport, my lady. At least, coming from where we are."

Lady Bernadette's smile widened into a grin. "And you two are masters of the game, is that it?"

"I'm better at it than Nottie, even though she is more quick-thinking than I. But she gets angry and then doesn't play well. I never get angry," Emmeline said with great seriousness. "Nottie sits on me if I become ill-mannered."

Clearly fascinated, Lady Bernadette leaned in. "I'm afraid I didn't play the game. I won by accident, I suppose?"

Emmeline nodded. "Exactly. But it still counts because you scored high romantically. It wouldn't do for everyone to play for love, or no important family alliances would ever happen." She held up one finger, like a teacher instructing a student. "However, the occasional romantic win gives the rest of the players hope. Do you see?"

"Amazing." Lady Bernadette shook her head. "Matthias and I sweetened the pot and I never even knew it." She tilted her head thoughtfully. "Now I'm passionately curious if he knew it." Then she narrowed her eyes at them, sharply focused once more. "So how does John Barton figure into this game? A Staffordshire vicar can't bring in very high points, can he?"

Norah was about to agree with her ladyship, but Emmeline giggled.

"He can when he's the son of the Bishop of Gloucester!"

Norah's head snapped around. She stared at Emmeline. "He is?"

Lady Bernadette nodded thoughtfully. "Yes, he is. I'd forgotten that. He never speaks of it."

"He told me the night I woke up," Emmeline said smugly.

He never said a word to me. All the talks they'd had and he'd never mentioned anything of his life before he came to Haven.

"Papa thinks it's a very acceptable alliance, politically," Emmeline went on. "And the way we met earns high romance points as well. It would be different if I weren't an heiress, of course. I'd have to look for someone a bit more well set."

Norah's stomach dropped. She'd thought Emmeline had only been flirting, spinning her web. Practicing.

Lady Bernadette seemed to be on the same track. "So are you seriously pursuing a proposal?"

"Papa said I should," Emmeline said calmly. "Papa has several investors in Gloucester and many political associates as well. There's much to be gained from such an alliance."

Norah barely heard her. Emmeline sounded quite decided.

"And I'll be twenty soon, so there really isn't a moment to waste."

"Lady Emmeline, aside from your father's machinations, how do you *feel* about John Barton?"

Norah's attention awoke. Yes, good question. She bit her lower lip waiting to hear Emmeline's response.

To her surprise, Emmeline blushed. "He's very handsome. I quite turn to butter when he takes my hand." Then she actually let out a wistful sigh. "I like him very much. He's so kind. I don't think I've ever met a man so kind."

So Emmeline did see John as a man and not just a target. Reassuring and horrifying at the same time. With her beauty and wealth? And then sincere liking as well? John Barton didn't stand a chance.

Norah frowned. "But what about Bertie?"

"Bertie?" Lady Bernadette widened her eyes.

"Lord Bertram Ardmore," Norah explained. "Some people call him Purty Bertie, for he is a bit of a dandy."

Emmeline smoothed a fold in her skirts. "Bertie wasn't serious about me. He was only passing the time."

Lord Bertram had seemed quite keen to Norah. He wasn't politically advantageous in himself, being more interested in fashion and his social life—much like Emmeline!—but his wealth and title could have been parlayed into useful connections. Uncle Bester had supported the match. Even Norah had been inclined to approve.

When Lord Bertram stopped calling upon Emmeline last season, Norah had assumed that Emmeline had discouraged him now that Kewell Abbey no longer needed his income. He was just one of many suitors and Emmeline seemed to forget him quickly.

Of course, Norah didn't blame Emmeline, for John Barton was much more handsome than Lord Bertram. As well as strong and kind and warm and honest...

He held me on the bridge.

I am in such a pickle.

Emmeline turned back to Lady Bernadette with a bright smile. "Don't you see? John would be family for certain then. Not simply a family friend!"

Lady Bernadette relaxed and smiled as well. "Yes, that would be wonderful." Somewhat wryly, she added, "I know Matthias would be over the moon with joy if John married."

Numbly, Norah wondered what solemn, brooding Lord Matthias looked like when he was over the moon with joy. Probably still solemn but slightly less brooding.

What would John Barton look like when he was over the moon with joy? As perhaps on his wedding day as he took his forever vows with England's most beautiful bride?

Norah felt ill. *I don't think I want to know.*

IT WAS A good thing Miss Higgins brewed such uncompromising tea, for before Norah was entirely free of the whiskey's embrace, there arose yet another ruckus.

A chambermaid dashed into Emmeline's chambers and hauled Lady Bernadette away at a run. Miss Higgins took a moment to check Emmeline's teeth for chocolate (she found none) and to assess Norah's ability to maneuver the stairs and speak coherently.

"Just keep your thoughts to yourself and only answer direct questions and you'll do fine, miss. And your hair still looks right nice." Miss Higgins glanced at Emmeline. "Extra pins you reckon, my lady?"

Emmeline nodded. "Simply loads."

Miss Higgins brushed a last few evergreen needles from Norah's gown. "My thanks for the hint, my lady. My Lady Bernadette's hair is a right trial, it is."

Miss Higgins pronounced them acceptable. "Now hurry on down to greet the new guests. Milady's aunt and uncle are here, a day late and dead tired I expect, so step quickly or you'll look like snobs for missing them when milady stuffs them into their beds for a nap."

As they hurried from Norah's chamber, Emmeline whispered to Norah, "I wonder if I could hire Higgins away from Havensbeck. I should enjoy such honesty, shouldn't you?"

Knowing that Emmeline didn't give much thought to the private lives of servants, Norah didn't bother to inform Emmeline that Miss Higgins would never leave Haven, or her tightknit family, or the certainty that she would find her true love at any moment.

Be careful what you wish for, Miss Higgins.

Despite their hurry, Norah stopped Emmeline at the top of the stairs. "You're serious? You, a country vicar's wife?"

Emmeline's eyes widened. "Goodness no! I should never want to take care of people all the time. So dull! Can you imagine?"

"No, no not even a little," Norah replied dryly. Emmeline had never been one to spot the irony in a situation.

Emmeline smiled like a mischievous child. "After all, he's only a vicar because he's poor. He won't need to do it anymore if he marries me. I have a lot of money now." With that, she danced ahead down the stairs.

Norah followed more slowly.

They made it to the front foyer just as Lord Matthias was carefully handing in a frail man in his seventies. An older woman, although not as old as the man, fluttered around them, fussing over the old fellow's snow-dusted shoulders and hat.

It's snowing. How lovely. For a moment Norah forgot and thought to tease John Barton outside for a ramble in the falling snow.

Cousin. He'll be my cousin, if Emmeline has her way.

And Emmeline always had her way.

Then John was there, rushing forward to take the lady's arm and give a gentle clap on the shoulder of the older fellow. He was smiling in true welcome and Norah recalled Miss Higgins's kindly gossip of how Lady Bernadette had grown up orphaned and poor, raised by her aunt and her uncle, who was vicar in a destitute parish south of Havensbeck.

And how a young curate had come to study with the vicar and had fallen in love with his mentor's pretty ward. Then had steadfastly waited until she grew up before setting out to court her, only to lose her to the handsome brooding widower, Lord Matthias.

High romance points indeed.

Norah endured the introductions, watched Emmeline tease a smile from the weary old fellow—was no man immune?—and stayed out of the way as the couple were divested of their winter wear.

Mostly, she watched John. His warm gaze shone with true affection for the elderly vicar and his anxious wife, until he and Lady Bernadette almost seemed to be the welcoming couple. Lord Matthias appeared to take such matters serenely enough, although Norah noticed that he tended to push Emmeline to stay at John's side.

Oh yes, Lord Matthias would definitely prefer that handsome John

Barton was happily married off, but his intent seemed equally as kindhearted as it was possessive. This made Norah like him even more.

Jasper appeared with a tray bearing a decanter of sherry and a tiny glass. Norah saw "Mrs. Vicar" protest without much conviction—and then quickly down two glasses "to fortify myself" before directing the tray to her room.

Of course, Uncle Bester, Great-Aunt Blythe and Mama were there in the welcoming party, but they all retreated to stand with Norah while the actual family welcomed the newcomers.

Simon pelted in from outside where he announced that the horses were safe and sound and the snow was coming down harder. Mrs. Vicar (Norah couldn't think of her as Mrs. Goodrich now. She blamed Jasper entirely for this.) fussed over Simon's snowy coat and boots in a motherly fashion until Norah realized the deep love that flowed beneath the fretful woman's antics.

They are so happy to be together.

Norah took Mama's hand and tucked her other arm into Uncle Bester's. She needed to remember that she had a family too, a family that loved her in their way. She had Emmeline, who was as close as a sister and Mama who, though timid and not deeply thoughtful, was devoted to her. *I may not be well-understood but I belong.* Not everyone in the world could lay claim to even that.

Perhaps it was too much to ask "magical" Haven for true love as well.

Chapter 12

J OHN FELT AS happy to see his old mentor and Mrs. Goodrich as he would have been to see his own parents. Happier actually, he admitted in the depths of his heart, for he held Isaiah and Sarah in bright affection, while his feelings for his mother and the Bishop bore the cloudier tinge of duty, obligation and failed expectations on both sides.

To be part of the joy of the moment, to be welcoming people who were the family of his heart, left John with a glow of contentment that he had not allowed himself for far too long, so wrapped up as he'd been in his unhappiness.

His gaze was caught by the Grey family standing just a little apart but smiling at the happiness of Lady Bernadette and Simon.

Lord Bester might remind John of his father on occasion, but that was not all bad. Lady Blythe and Mrs. Grey were kindness and consideration itself. As for Miss Norah Grey, he'd thought they were friends.

At that moment, Miss Grey caught his eye and gave him a small embarrassed smile and a rueful little shrug. *What a mess! Let's hope everyone forgets!*

John felt a foolish grin take over his face, so relieved was he that she wasn't angry with him any longer.

Lady Emmeline came to stand beside him. "What a happy party we shall be this Christmas! We have so much to be thankful for!"

John turned to smiled down at her, struck anew by her perfection, as he always was. She truly did have a good and kindly nature beneath it as well. He should not be put off by the way she sometimes recalled to mind the spoiled society girls his parents had pressed upon him.

Was that why he'd originally decided so definitively upon Bernadette? Because she was the opposite of everything he'd been pressured to want?

Unfair to Bernadette if it were true—and unfair to Lady Emmeline as well. John vowed to himself to simply take the Greys and Lady Emmeline for exactly who they showed themselves to be and allow no assumptions to color his perception. After all, Miss Norah Grey loved them all and she seemed to John to be a most astute judge of character.

Tucking Lady Emmeline's hand into his elbow, John turned to smile at the Greys and particularly Norah.

But Miss Norah Grey was turning away.

THAT EVENING, JOHN could not help but notice that neither Lady Emmeline nor Miss Grey ventured down to the dining room for dinner. It was a lively party for all that. Vicar Goodrich and Lord Bester had many mutual acquaintances, hard as that was to believe, and both had a passionate interest in politics, although perhaps more opposed than united. Still, both fellows were amiable in their discourse and all in all it was an interesting debate.

Sarah Goodrich and the Grey ladies cozied up to the fire after dinner in the retiring room, while Jasper plied them with rather astonishing levels of sherry and dainty sweets from Cook. John had the impression that they were talking about him. Whenever he looked their way, they seemed to just be turning away.

Matthias and Bernadette moved through the room, seeing to everyone's tiniest comfort. John felt a genial fondness for them both. Of course, that could have been his lordship's rather astonishing brandy.

After many months of bread and cheese and cold roast—minus the parsnips—and seeing to his own fires, John had to admit that the finer things were, well, finer. He had embraced rebuilding the vicarage himself, but was forced to admit that it would be lovely to sit down to an excellent meal and a good glass of liquor and the company of someone who wasn't himself or Simon Goodrich (who was even now avoiding bedtime by hiding behind Vicar Goodrich's chair and pretending great interest in politics).

It was too bad that Lady Emmeline and Miss Grey hadn't felt up to the evening. Lady Emmeline, Bernadette informed him, had overdone herself just a bit and had regenerated her headache. This was normal, she added, according to the physician. It might continue off and on for several weeks.

On Miss Grey's condition, Bernadette was more close-mouthed. If Norah felt anywhere near as much bruising from their incident as he did, John could well understand her taking to her bed. Still, he was worried about her.

And Lady Emmeline, of course.

He became restless without their company. In the end, he caught Jasper's attention. "Do you think I should attend the young ladies before it grows too late? Perhaps with a tray of hot cocoa and some of these?" He indicated the plate that was even now on its way to the elder ladies. It was full of tiny jewel-toned pastries and little jellied things. The entire tray wouldn't slow a man down for more than three minutes, but it seemed that ladies liked to nibble away at more dainty things.

Jasper eyed him thoughtfully for a moment. "Why yes, sir. I think it would be very helpful if you looked in on our convalescents. Being the vicar and all, of course. They are spending a quiet hour or two in Lady Emmeline's sitting room. You should go on. I'll have a tray sent up straightaway."

Suddenly energized by the thought of such congenial company, John found he had to restrain himself from taking the stairs two at a time.

Even so, he arrived at Lady Emmeline's door only seconds ahead of young Brand and Tanner, both loaded with steaming pots of chocolate and trays of absolutely miniature food. It looked like a feast meant for some very wealthy mice. John shook his head. Matthias's cook was a true craftsman but the very sight of all those tiny, jammy things made John long for a thick steak and a foamy ale.

Miss Higgins answered John's tap and only slightly raised her brows at his somewhat lame excuse of "checking on my injured flock."

"Well, if that's what ye wish to call it, Vicar. The ladies are just sittin' and readin'."

John nodded. "I like reading!" *Good Lord, I am such a gubbins.*

Miss Higgins turned away and John could hear her murmuring to the ladies. She opened the door again. "The ladies will see you, Vicar. Mind you don't keep them up too late nor be too jolly. Lady Emmeline is right headachey this eve."

John said something inane about being quiet company and then he was allowed within with his beasts of jammy burden in tow.

NORAH ONLY GLANCED up at John Barton for a moment as he entered, just long enough to nod a greeting in what she hoped was a congenial manner, and then she looked back down at the book she was reading aloud to Emmeline.

He took the chair opposite her and sat quietly, thankfully not interrupting her with banal greetings.

Her voice remained smooth enough and her hands barely shook as she turned the pages. It was astonishing how the pounding of her pulse alerted no one to her dire condition. The ache in her chest was a silent cry and the blurring of her vision didn't matter, for she'd read this collection of poems to Emmeline so many times that she knew them by heart.

"Snow in thy heart and chill in thy soul,

May it melt before the fire of mine love.

And whilst thee dream, mine words cajole

A southern wind to the wings of thine north-bound dove."

Her voice caught in her throat at those words. Norah paused to pick up the cup young Mr. Brand had poured for her before he left. She took a casual sip of her chocolate and let the bitter richness distract her from her hammering heart.

Vicar Barton did nothing to ruin the silence, so Norah allowed the book to close in her lap. A glance at Emmeline assured Norah that her cousin had fallen asleep to escape the throb in her head. Miss Higgins was all abustle in the bedchamber off the sitting room, tending to something apparently more urgent than chaperoning two young ladies sitting with a vicar.

Norah leaned back a little in her chair. There seemed no point to maintaining perfect manners before a man who had already seen her at her shrewish worst. Would he ruin everything by mentioning it? No, he was surely too considerate for that.

Sipping the chocolate gave her something to do. Casting her gaze anywhere but at the man sitting opposite her, she spotted a tray of ornamental treats. Her belly chose that moment to growl into the silence.

John Barton snorted. Norah rolled her eyes at her own absurdity and let simple laughter loose, a gentle chuckle in the hush.

"I suppose now I'll not be able to refuse to eat those crown jewels on a plate."

He smiled and rose. Taking the tray in one hand, he held his other behind his back and bowed like Jasper. "A tiny morsel of utmost artistry, Miss Grey?"

Norah sighed. "It's that or put them under glass for future generations to admire." She chose something that looked like a ruby on a golden disc and popped it in her mouth. Her eyes widened. "Raspberry tart?"

The vicar—for she must continue to think of him as the vicar!—gazed perplexed at the tray. "Then why not simply make a raspberry tart that looks like a raspberry tart?"

Norah shook her head. "It's a mystery to me, sir. I like to eat proper food. This plate makes me want a bit of toasted cheese on bread."

"Steak and ale," he murmured.

Still, they tried some more. They even made Miss Higgins come in to taste a selection, for Norah dared not send the tray back uneaten. "The poor man worked so hard!"

Soon enough, the array of dainties was reduced to crumbs. Emmeline never woke to partake, but Norah assured her conscience that Emmeline preferred chocolates and had already had a double serving of those earlier in the day.

Miss Higgins agreed that the ornate tray was "right silly" even as she popped the last ruby-raspberry tart into her mouth and returned to her tasks, wiping her hands on her apron.

Norah had to admit to herself that the impractical, beautiful food had been incredibly satisfying. She must remember to compliment the cook.

John Barton sat back with a sigh. "I'd never have believed it. The man is a mad genius." He shook his head and gave Norah a tranquil, overfed smile. "Every day I think, 'What a day I've had!' and then I think the next day will be terribly dull in comparison." His smile widened. "Things are never dull around you, are they?"

Norah looked away. "I'm the most ordinary person in the world." She smoothed her skirts and then, restless under his gaze, stood to brandish the poker at the fire though it did not need it.

"I think you are a very odd person, actually. You are an oyster, shut up tightly, never letting anyone see the pearl within." He shook his finger at her. "But I've cracked you, you see."

You have shattered me, in fact, sir. She was heart-sore from these past days with him. She forced a calm smile and turned the conversation from herself.

"You are not Staffordshire-born, Vicar Barton. From whence do you originate? Do I hear a hint of Gloucester in your speech?" It was cheating, but Norah still stung from his secrecy with her while telling Emmeline everything. And it took his attention away from her own secrets.

"You are correct," he said.

"Yet you chose this place to settle, far from your home."

His cheerful confectionary daze seemed to recede and he frowned into the fire. "I'm fond of my city and the people, yet ..." He seemed to struggle for a moment. Then, he shook his head. "My mother is a good woman but not a demonstrative sort. She takes her cues from my father most of the time. I barely left a mark on my home despite all the years of my life there. I was an ill-favored child. I fear my parents were more likely to hide me than to parade me before their associates."

This Norah could scarcely believe. Her doubt must have shown in her expression for he shook his head ruefully. "It is truth. In a house absolutely chock-full of family portraits, there are none of me. My father had little interest in me at all until I did well in seminary school. Then suddenly, no detail of my life escaped his notice. Alas, his hopes were doomed to be dashed. He believes me to be his single egregious failure. I was meant to follow in his footsteps, you see, likely long before I was even conceived."

"Do you mean choosing the Church?" Norah couldn't see how a bishop could regret it when his son chose the same as he had.

"Ah, but I do not serve the Church. Not the way he meant for me to. I am a country vicar. I serve the people of Haven and Havensbeck. At this distance, I am as far from whom my father wishes as I could possibly be."

"Your father is the Bishop of Gloucester. You grew up in the bishop's palace." Norah marveled. He made it sound cheerless and intimidating. She imagined a silent, lonely, perfectly-dressed little boy, quelled by his domineering father, oppressed by the grandeur of his surroundings. Then she thought of shabby little Arthur Tanner, free to throw snowballs and slump on muddy steps, suffering loss but with his loving family knit tightly to him in his time of grief. "Emmeline told me."

He only blinked. "Yes. Didn't I say?"

"No, actually, you didn't. You only spoke of Haven, the Higgins family, your choir and young Simon Goodrich. It is as if you didn't live before you landed here."

He nodded. "I suppose it's because I didn't. I tried to be someone my father would respect, but in time I came to see that he might be the one missing the point of church work."

"How can that be? He's the Bishop!"

John leaned forward with his hands clasped, as if he really cared whether she understood.

"I appreciate that someone needs to run matters. The Church of England is a vast organization, with needs in England itself and in far-flung parts of the world. Gloucester is an old and powerful parish. It has influence all the way up to the throne. My father is a responsible leader and a fierce defender of his parish—but it is no sacrifice to him. He loves the power, loves the challenge and control, but not the meaning behind it." He shrugged and leaned back. "My father almost never speaks to someone who isn't a high officer of the Church or a member of Parliament. He never eats plain good food off a wooden plate in a rustic kitchen nor weds young lovers nor hammers a nail nor holds someone's hand when they're dying. I sometimes think he is the one who is wasting his life, not I."

Oh, my poor heart. He is wonderful. She'd been so suspicious of his attraction to Emmeline. She was now realizing that he was, in fact, a secret romantic. An errant knight looking for his grand quest.

He looked up at her then and seemed taken aback by her expression.

Norah quickly turned away. "I suppose it is time Miss Higgins and I put Emmeline to bed. It can't be good for her head to lay upon a stuffed chair—"

"Oh, no you don't! Your story now, Miss Grey. I will lie down upon this carpet and sing 'Good King Wenceslas' at the top of my lungs until you do. I have an excellent baritone."

The laughter in his voice tweaked at her tattered nerves. He had no notion of what his friendly attention did to her. Norah turned on him. "I will not be bullied. Besides, I'm much better at intimidation than you, for I've had years of practice while you've kept busy being kind and good."

He glanced at sleeping, angelic Emmeline and smirked at her. "Oh yes, I can tell your life has been a right trial."

Oh, just you wait, Vicar Barton! Marriage to "delicate little Emmeline" would be a life of tug-of-war. She would almost enjoy watching him drown in his own assumptions, if it wouldn't hurt so much.

However, she did owe him something, for he'd been unguarded with her. She knotted her fingers a little before she opened doors in her memory that she tried not to walk through anymore. "Even before I ever met Emmeline, I had to manage my mother. She's a darling person but she hasn't an ounce of good sense. She married my father in a whirlwind romance and elopement. They had perhaps been drinking, the story has it. Somehow they ended up over the border in Scotland and wed in Gretna Green before anyone ever noticed they were missing."

"But that's romantic, isn't it? Most young ladies would think so."

"Most young ladies don't have to watch their father be disowned and stripped of his title and entailment. Yes, it can happen if the baron is a good friend of the Prince Regent and is better at cards than His Highness. My father took it as a sign to be as irresponsible as possible. By the time I was ten years of age, he spent more time in a bottle than with his wife and child. One night he thought it a grand idea to drink himself into racing his horse in full dark. He fell, of course, at great speed." She sat down abruptly, her knees giving out under the cascade of memory and loss.

"He wasn't a strong man, but I adored him. On the few nights he was not out drinking, he would teach me to play chess by the fire. I was only a child and he seemed the most handsome, brave, dashing father anyone could want. Looking back I realize that he was lost to himself. He never knew who he was after his fall from grace. It's only too bad that he couldn't find himself as a husband and father."

She dashed at her damp eyes. "Silly of me. It all happened so long ago that it seems as if it is someone else's story that I tell."

Her hand was enveloped in two warm ones. Her thudding heart took her back to the moment John Barton had held her on the bridge. She knew that moment had been only a gesture of his innate kindness and goodness and that he had meant simply to be a good friend, a strong shoulder. She didn't weave romantic fantasies around it, for to read anything but kindness into it would be unjust to him and tarnish the purity of the moment itself.

So she left her hand in his and took his compassion as it was given. Perhaps it was her due, for all it had happened so long ago.

"Mama was utterly shattered. I couldn't get her to rise from her bed. Our cook left and our manservant took the little silver we had as payment on back wages. There wasn't anything I could do to stop him. Finally, Mama revived from her grief enough to realize that the house was cold and dark and the bread I'd been bringing her was moldy." Poor Mama had been horrified. "She sent a letter to Uncle Bester, my father's elder brother."

"Good Lord! How long did she lie abed?"

Norah didn't want him to think badly of Mama. Poor pretty, impractical Mama, who could have been the mold that cast Emmeline. "A few months. It wasn't her fault. She wasn't strong either. She loves him still, you know. They were simply ... unlucky for each other."

"You lost him, too. Did anyone care for your grief?"

Norah shook her head. "I was fine. I'm always fine. I'm built of something different. There are people who are like fine crystal. Beautiful and precious and easily shattered. I'm made of something much more common. Wood, perhaps. Or maybe stone."

His hands squeezed hers. "I heard you with Artie Tanner today. You aren't even a wee bit like stone." His fingers touched her chin and she had to lift her head to meet his gaze. "Wood, now... yes, I see the forest in those eyes of yours. Green and brown, full of life and birdsong and the rushing wind in the treetops." He smiled. "I work with wood every day, you realize. One has to know what one is doing with wood and take great care, for if cut wrong it is ruined." His hands sprang wide, like a piece of wood splitting apart. "Even strong wood can break, Miss Grey, if one does not take care."

Norah took advantage of the moment to pull away slightly, taking her hands back. John Barton in the dim, candle-lit room, virtually alone with her, was too much, too intimate and far too comfortable. She would be compelled to say something starry-eyed and humiliating and confessional at any moment. Then he would still be kind and still be friendly, but he would be so very gentle, so very careful, so very *sorry* to have encouraged her. That pity would burn as hot as revulsion would.

She looked down at her hands clasped safely over her midriff. "That's very kind of you to say, Vicar Barton. Perhaps you're right. It's merely a flight of fancy anyway." Standing and stepping back and turning toward sleeping Emmeline put a safe distance between them. "If you'll excuse us, Vicar Barton, it's past time Lady Emmeline went to her bed."

"Call me John," he said quickly. "If you will."

She cast him a quick smile of regret over her shoulder. "Oh no. That is not a possibility, Vicar Barton."

He had to go then, although he looked mightily confused. "Then I should bid you goodnight."

Norah answered him quickly and automatically until he left. The door shut at last. She gave Emmeline's shoulder a shake. It didn't work. "Oh, Emmeline, do wake up. I can't carry you and Miss Higgins will try and probably hurt herself in doing so. Up you go, or I'll call Uncle Bester to lift you."

That sufficed, as it always did. Emmeline might have her father wrapped around her pinkie finger, but that didn't mean that the effort to do so wasn't exhausting in itself.

Norah put Emmeline to bed with a cool cloth on her head and tiptoed off to her own room. Vicar Barton had seemed to have something else to say and Norah could not bear to hear another word from him tonight, so she slipped silently through the door of her own bedchamber before he could hear her from his.

Leaning her back against the wood and listening to her heart break in the silence of her dark room was like the snap of a tree branch overcome by the cruelty of an ice storm.

I like him.

It wasn't the right word. She knew the right word, but she dared not give in to that word. That word was never meant for someone like her.

I love him.

Oh. Well, now I've done it.

How was she supposed to fall out of love with the man her cousin meant to marry?

Chapter 13

C HRISTMAS EVE ARRIVED two days later with the clatter of eager footmen and giggling maids and Emmeline dancing next to Norah's bedside, up on tiptoes in her excitement for the ball that evening. The last few days of calm and rest had done her much good.

Sadly, that was not the case with Norah. She rubbed blurry eyes. She hadn't been sleeping well at all lately. Perhaps it was the way she spent the last two days tiptoeing down the halls, peering around corners, snatching bits of this and that to eat on the run, all in the cause of carefully avoiding the vicar. Such tension wore at her nerves. Yet she so dreaded to be drawn into a "friendly" conversation for fear she would spew out passionate declarations and fling herself into his arms. Her love filled her, stretching her skin painfully to contain it. One prick, one tiny cut, and she would gush her feelings like a burst dam.

Seeing him was too painful. Not seeing him was more painful still. She had caught a glimpse of him outside once, playing about in the snow with young Simon, flinging snowballs at each other like brothers. She'd pressed herself to the window, standing high and crouching low, her gaze following him like a hunting cat.

Last evening, she'd followed him with Emmeline on his arm as they walked through the gallery with Miss Higgins trailing a permissive distance behind. Norah couldn't hear his words but he'd used his storytelling voice so she assumed he was giving away all sorts of interesting tidbits regarding the Havensbeck ancestors as he showed Emmeline the portraits.

Emmeline, on the other hand, while not averse to spending time with Vicar Barton, seemed more interested in creating a sensation at the ball tonight in her newest and finest gown. Surely no one from the backside of nowhere that was Haven knew the first thing about Lementeur, other than Lady Bernadette and Lord Matthias, but Emmeline was going to be appearing as "Lady Mariana's Heiress" before his lordship and she felt the need to make an impression.

Being carried into Havensbeck Manor unconscious and bleeding was going to be difficult to top, but Emmeline seemed determined to try.

"We must go to the milliner's," Emmeline stated firmly. "I don't like my hair ribbons. There's something not quite right about them."

Since Em's hair ornaments were from Lementeur, as were her gowns, Norah seriously doubted any such lack. Emmeline was prone to fits of meticulousness when it came to beauty and grooming, so Norah knew it would do no good to argue.

She arose with a groan. Best to get it over with. However, that didn't mean she couldn't do a bit of bargaining. "There's something you must do for me first."

EMMELINE HALTED AT the stairs down to the kitchens. "I mustn't stay long. The steam will make my hair simply hideous."

Norah patted Emmeline's hand. "Dearest, you couldn't be hideous if you wore a mud-covered flour sack with a crown of dead fish in your hair." Her sisterly touch turned into a implacable grip. She hauled Emmeline onward. "Now, come on!"

All Emmeline had to do was to declare ardent gratitude to the cook for the chocolates, which she did with fervent sincerity, and the many other beautiful trays which had been sent up. Then she only needed to stand there and look beseeching and heartbroken while Norah informed the man of the dire plight facing the Tanner family, who only lacked a pudding to ease their terrible grief.

She needn't have rehearsed it so diligently, although it was always good to get Emmeline's lines just right. The cook practically shoved the pudding at them while never taking his enraptured gaze from Emmeline. Norah gently suggested that one of the footmen should deliver it, for Lady Emmeline could hardly be expected to throw it over her shoulder and tramp through knee-high snow to the Tanner farm.

"Oh, yes! So much like Lady Marianna! Anything, my lady, anything for you!"

It was always easier to get one's way when one was beautiful. They left the love-struck felloe mooning over Emmeline.

"Another conquest. He's going to feed you up like an Easter lamb." Norah cheerfully poked Emmeline in the belly. "Baa-aah!"

Emmeline slapped her hand away, then grinned. "That was fun. I can't believe you know all these things about the local people already."

Norah only forced a smile and shook her head. She couldn't very well tell Emmeline that she'd fallen in love with Haven even as she'd fallen in love with Haven's vicar.

HAVENSBECK MANOR WAS in a tizzy. There was no other word for it. What had been a sort of organized chaos for the last several days was now a whirling maelstrom of running maids, galloping footmen, Lady Bernadette flying from one crisis to another, and Lord Matthias striding to and fro, trying to handle some of the arrangements for the ball but mostly bellowing for his wife.

Fortunately, the elder guests decided to take a late breakfast in their rooms and settle in for a restful afternoon before the evening's more strenuous activities.

That left Emmeline and Norah to their own devices. Even Miss Higgins was called away by her ladyship. Emmeline, having been promised a trip into the village by Norah and ever more distressed about the perfection of her ribbons, quite frankly wanted out of the tizzy house.

Norah couldn't have agreed more. She dashed off a note to Lady Bernadette regarding their destination and pressed it into the hand of the first maid who scuttled past Emmeline's door.

They'd made it all the way to the foyer and were tying on their bonnets when Jasper came rushing up, breathless and flushed.

"Milady says 'You must wait for your escort because the doctor told me that Lady Emmeline isn't to be allowed out at all and even though she isn't a prisoner, she must not exert herself with a long walk in the cold weather'."

Norah was quite certain Jasper was repeating Lady Bernadette's speech word for word. She could almost hear the other woman's breathless efficiency.

Jasper went on in his own words. "And she's quite right, too, Lady Emmeline. What if the exertion causes you to take another headache?

You wouldn't want to miss the ball!"

That was enough to convince Emmeline and Norah was rather chagrined that she'd not taken Emmeline's injury into account. She didn't mind taking a cart and having an escort, as long as it wasn't—

Vicar John Barton galloped youthfully down the stairs into the foyer. "Good day, Lady Emmeline, Miss Grey! Lady Bernadette asked me to take you into Haven for the afternoon."

No one noticed Norah's sudden reluctance but Emmeline, who only gave her a quick elbow in the side as she smiled up at Vicar Barton.

"Why thank you, sir! We should very much enjoy your company today. And you may be our guide, for I do not know where to find Haven's milliner."

"It is across from the confectionary shop," Norah and John said simultaneously. Norah saw him smile at her, his expression amused and conspiratorial. She nodded distantly and looked down to adjust the wrist button of her kidskin gloves.

Emmeline's eyes brightened further. "Well, I don't particularly care for sweets, but Norah does!"

The vicar smiled warmly at Emmeline. "Then we must stop there as well."

"I just wish it was someone else," Norah whispered to Emmeline as they turned away to head out of doors.

Emmeline shrugged as she spread her fingers wide into the perfectly-fitted confines of her ermine-trimmed gloves. "What difference does it make who drives us?" Clearly Em was more concerned with their release from the manor than with their escort. Emmeline had been confined for more than a week and now wanted *out*. Their driver could have been anyone, clearly.

The fact that Emmeline wasn't particularly excited by the prospect of riding on the cart seat next to her suitor meant something, Norah was certain of it. She simply couldn't think past the jangling of her nerves to figure out what it was.

Just as they were ready to depart, Lady Bernadette dashed into the foyer, running full tilt with her skirts in both hands, like a country girl late to milk the cows. That, along with her flyaway hair and pink cheeks, made Norah remember that Lady Bernadette had likely milked an actual cow or two in her life. Astonishing.

Norah felt a bit envious of her ladyship's varied assembly of skills.

"Oh, thank goodness. You haven't left yet. John, when you return I shall need you to go over your performance schedule again. I'm sorry. I know you've told me and I wrote it down, I know I did! Norah, you're to stop everything and bring Emmeline directly home if she has even the slightest headache!" Then Lady Bernadette turned to smile warmly at Emmeline. "Cook told me what you did this morning, Lady Emmeline. I just wanted to thank you for being so thoughtful to the Tanner family. I cannot bear to think that I forgot about Mrs. Tanner—but I think I did. I'm pleased and proud that you took care of the matter of the pudding for me!"

John nearly interrupted to correct Lady Bernadette. It had been Norah Grey, had it not? Then he saw Miss Grey nodding and smiling and looking proudly at her cousin.

He'd been so wrong. Miss Grey was not the slightest bit envious of Lady Emmeline. In fact, her support of her much-more-fortunate cousin seemed absolutely stalwart.

John realized then that she was not at all jealous or small-minded. He couldn't believe he had ever thought so. She clearly loved her cousin and was Lady Emmeline's fiercest advocate.

That was a good thing, was it not?

It was only when John saw Lady Emmeline blush demurely and bask in Lady Bernadette's praise that he felt an inkling of unease. Surely it would be the more generous thing to share the credit with Miss Grey, who had discovered the matter in the first place? Yet he liked Emmeline. He liked all the Greys. Emmeline's father was so hearty and warm. Kindly Lady Blythe's humor was sharp as a needle. Norah's sweet and eccentric mother was an innocent soul. Norah— Miss Grey was very good with her, firmly but gently keeping her mother's wandering conversation and sometimes even her actual physical path somewhat straight. The Greys seemed such an affectionate family.

John had always wanted one of those.

Then Lady Emmeline turned a dazzling smile upon him and John forgot his misgivings at the dizzying sensation of being the focus of her exquisite attention.

What was it Miss Grey had said to him?

"I'm astonished at your incredible intelligence and devastated by your manly, manly muscles. Please, tell me every mundane detail about yourself because you are endlessly fascinating to me—and I'll pretend not to notice that you never, ever ask me a single thing about what I like or long for, or heaven knows, what I actually really think about anything."

That was precisely how Lady Emmeline gazed at him now, as if he was the most wonderful being she'd ever encountered. Even though he now understood that it was mostly an effective bit of theater, he could still feel it working on him. He'd never thought of himself of being a gullible male before, defenseless against the wiles of a pretty woman. He'd seen it happen, but it always seemed to happen to some other fellow.

Poor Lady Emmeline. How exhausting it must be to be her.

John felt quite protective suddenly. He smiled gently back at her and held out his arm. "Tell me, Lady Emmeline, do you prefer summertime or winter?"

She blinked in surprise at his question, which did much to interrupt the blinding glamor of her smile, thank Heaven. To his surprise, she spent a serious moment considering the question.

"I prefer summer, I believe. Yes, definitely summer. I suppose it is because summers are full of parties and balls, and I dearly love to dance." She smiled much more naturally as she tucked her arm into his and strolled out the door with him. "Yet, here we are in the middle of winter and we shall all dance tonight, even Great-Aunt Blythe!"

John laughed. "A very well considered answer, my lady."

He was aware that Miss Grey had followed them to where John's heavy-wheeled cart and stolid, thick-legged mule awaited them, held by a horse groom who jiggled a little in the cold air. John approved. His mule was a creature who would never shy at a little whirlwind.

When he handed Miss Grey up to the seat after seating Lady Emmeline, she nodded and thanked him with downcast eyes. He noticed that she removed her hand from his as quickly as possible.

John wasn't certain what was wrong with Miss Grey. She didn't seem precisely ill, and when Lady Emmeline spoke to her, she answered her cousin readily enough. Yet every time John spoke to her, she looked somewhere over his left shoulder and answered as briefly as possible, in a tone just short of indifferent.

Whatever caused her mood, John did not intrude. They'd had a nice evening a few days ago, sharing a plate of dainty food and talking so comfortably. Yet he'd scarcely spoken to her since.

Whenever his mind traveled back to that evening—as it did rather a lot—one particular thing kept snagging his memory.

He's spontaneously asked her to call him John. He didn't really know why, except that he'd felt they were friends at that moment. She'd cast him a strangely unreadable look.

"Oh no. That is not a possibility, Vicar Barton."

He'd wanted to ask her what she meant ever since. What was not a possibility? Saying his given name? Being the friend of a country vicar? It was true that she came from a very good family, despite her father's unfortunate circumstance (about which John didn't care one whit). Yet his origins were nearly as good and besides, she hadn't seemed the sort to care even if they weren't. She took meals to Higgins-the-driver and shared her treats with Higgins-the-maid, so he knew quite well that she was no snob.

What made their friendship so impossible?

As he drove, Lady Emmeline chattered on amiably beside him, commenting on the passing scenery. John tumbled the question over and over in his mind, wearing away at the sharp corners. He felt the answer lay somewhere in his past encounters with Miss Grey, but he simply couldn't dig the key out of his memory.

"Oh! This is where I fell, isn't it?"

Startled, John pulled his mule to a stop. Egad, he'd rumbled Lady Emmeline right up the site of her terrible accident without a bit of warning! What was wrong with him? "How thoughtless of me! My deepest apologies, Lady Emmeline! I ought to have told you we would have to pass this way."

Lady Emmeline gazed at the stone wall for a long moment. "I want to look down."

"Em," Miss Grey murmured. "Please don't."

"Go on, Nottie," Lady Emmeline insisted. "Hop down and let me off. I want to see."

Miss Grey obeyed before John could make it round the cart to assist her. He handed Lady Emmeline down. She looked very fragile with her fur cloak wound around her, almost like a little girl wearing something of her mother's. She took a deep breath and picked her way through the snow to the wall. It was waist high on John, so she had to go on her tiptoes to see over its thickness to the river below. "I don't see the cracks the falling horse made."

"They've frozen over again, dear heart," Miss Grey murmured.

John examined Miss Grey for any sign of her previous disquiet, but other than a slight trembling of the hand she laid on her cousin's shoulder, she showed no fear. *Good for you, Norah.*

"Well, that is indeed very far to fall." Lady Emmeline turned to flash a cheerful smile at John. "I'm very glad you were there to catch me, Vicar John Barton!" Then, dusting the snow from her gloves with the air of finishing a task, she made her way back to the cart and waited for John to help her up.

John could only stare at Lady Emmeline's entirely unconcerned response to the scene of her almost-death.

Beside him, Miss Grey sighed. "She doesn't remember," she murmured. "After all, she was unconscious during almost the entire thing."

John turned to see those deep-forest eyes looking his way at last. Among the new shadows he saw there, he also found the fellowship forged when they had worked together to save lives.

So she had not forgotten.

Knowing it made him feel better, even though after that single shared moment she retreated back into the isolated place where she clearly did not want him to follow.

The three of them rode the rest of the way into Haven in thoughtful silence.

Chapter 14

H AVING ARRIVED AT the central square of Haven and turned the stolid mule over to the blacksmith for a warm wait in one of the smithy stalls, Norah was nearly wild with the need to escape the presence of the handsome couple. Emmeline was positively basking in the attention of her hero and John gazed down at Emmeline with warmth and tranquil appreciation.

He wasn't even being sickening, the way most men were when Emmeline was twining them around her finger. He was simply very good to her and Em clearly liked and admired him.

So why did Norah feel like screaming at them both?

"Oh look, the sweets shop! I adore sweets! Go on without me, I'll catch up in a moment!" She was being strange and she knew it, but it didn't stop her from actually fleeing their perfectly perfect perfectness. She blew into the shop and leaned against the shut door, her eyes shut tight and her heart aching.

"Ahem. May I help you, Miss Grey?"

Norah opened her eyes to see a pretty young woman in a spotless apron behind the counter. There was something familiar about her pert nose...

"You must be a Higgins."

The woman—or possibly girl, for when she smiled she looked no more than seventeen—nodded excitedly. "Yes, miss! I am! Did my auntie tell you about me?"

Auntie? Miss Higgins?

Norah shook her head, blinking at the sheer breadth of the Higgins dynasty. So many children. A stab of envy jabbed her directly between her ribs.

Getting ahold of herself, she straightened from her ridiculous pose against the door. "It's very nice to meet you, Miss Higgins—"

"Oh no miss!" The girl giggled. "I'm Mrs. Felton. Did you see the sign above the door? Felton's Sweets. My Ronnie's da owns the shop."

A husband, at her age? Norah suddenly felt every year of her spinsterdom like a wide stretch of desert before her.

Why do I mind? I don't even like the notion of marriage!

Dotty Auntie Nottie was still her destiny and she'd best get used to it. She stared at the rows of jars filled with bit of sugary color. They reminded her of the trays of jellies, and sitting in the firelight with Vicar Barton, sharing their shadowed histories.

Call me John.

She shook off the spell of memory and forced a smile for the dewy Mrs. Feldon. "I'd like to buy something that the children of Haven favor especially."

ACROSS THE SQUARE, John waited patiently for Lady Emmeline to purchase every green, blue-green, and yellow-green ribbon in the establishment. The milliner, Mrs. Corbin, was ecstatic.

"I bought up too many yards, Vicar," she confessed to John quietly. "It right worried me with the ball tonight and me havin' so much left unsold."

"Well, Lady Emmeline is a keen patron of—of fashion, I've noticed."

"Oh, aye! Isn't she a grand picture? Like a princess come to our little village of Haven." She gave John a wink. "A princess needs herself a knight in shining armor, Vicar, don't ye reckon?"

It seemed a strange thing to say. John merely smiled benignly and wondered to where Miss Grey had disappeared.

When John and Emmeline left the milliner's, with John toting an astonishingly large paper parcel packed with nothing but ribbon, they spotted Miss Grey leaving Felton's sweet shop with an even larger bundle of something that could only be sweets. John smiled. Miss Grey did love her confections.

"Oh, we're done already." Lady Emmeline sighed. "It's hours until we need to get ready for the ball. I don't want to go back to the manor yet."

Knowing that she'd spent much of the last week abed, John couldn't blame Lady Emmeline for her resistance to returning.

Miss Grey looked as if she wouldn't mind leaving half an hour ago, or even as if she hadn't come at all. Something in John rose to the challenge of impressing her. "May I give you ladies a tour of the vicarage?"

Miss Grey bit her bottom lip. Lady Emmeline didn't hesitate. "Yes! Excellent notion, sir! I'm absolutely perishing to see the vicarage!"

SOMEHOW VICAR JOHN Barton had tiptoed into Norah's dreams and built the very house for which she had always wished. It was achingly familiar and simultaneously surprising, the way that the windows were wide and tall and the daylight fell just so upon the floors. How she would have arranged the parlor just the same, and how the graceful curve of the banister leading up the stairs fit beneath her hand as if she'd used it all her life.

Emmeline didn't hesitate to peek into the mostly empty bedchambers, so Norah did as well. She saw the one meant to be a cozy nursery and she ached to see it filled. She glimpsed a single wide, curtained bed and blushed for the next ten minutes, for she would have chosen those very same rich blue jacquard draperies herself for the pleasure of seeing the firelight cast a glow of perfect evening light behind the privacy of their folds.

Emmeline was less impressed. "You'll be painting all this wooden paneling, I assume?"

John's voice was warm but firm. "I like the wood. I cut the paneling just that way to show off the grain."

Emmeline was flabbergasted. "You. You cut the wood. Did you built this house? With your actual hands?"

Norah felt her heart beat faster yet. She stroked her fingertips over the silky finish of the warm oak doorframe and shivered slightly. She didn't have to ask if he'd done it himself. He'd done it all with those strong, capable hands. She could see him everywhere, feel him in every square foot. It was part of him.

Emmeline's voice broke the spell. "But she works for you! She should cook them!"

Norah tried to ignore her thudding heart and followed Emmeline's voice—it was her irritated voice, oddly enough—down the back stairs to the cellar.

She found Emmeline and the vicar standing amid heaping bushel baskets of ... parsnips? Yes, parsnips. Hundreds of them, stored most improperly too, if she was not mistaken. Some would be rotting underneath, although at the moment the chill was keeping the cellar air sweet enough.

Emmeline turned to Norah, pulling her into what had clearly become a debate. "Nottie, his Higgins brings him raw parsnips and just leaves them that way!"

Vicar Barton looked amused and a little sheepish. He shrugged and smiled at Norah. "I've never had the heart to tell Mrs. Higgins that I don't know how to cook. She'll just want to do it for me, but she already works so hard. I'm sure it's dead simple, but as I cannot yet brew a decent pot of tea, it is quite beyond me. I think I'm a little bit defective in the kitchen."

Norah couldn't help but find the secret cache of guilty parsnips adorable.

I'm so smitten that I would likely find a random roomful of badgers adorable.

"Of course you cannot cook! The very idea!" Emmeline was incensed at the notion. "That's what Higgins is for!"

Norah saw John's eyelids flicker at the way Emmeline said "Higgins" without the more respectful (and honestly less confusing within the territory of Haven) title of "Mrs." It wasn't Emmeline's fault. In her world, no one called servants by anything but their surname.

Lord Bester found Norah's habit of using "Miss" or "Mister" quaint and somewhat seditious. Still, he acknowledged Norah's friendship with mere staff to be useful in certain situations, as when they needed to be cajoled into staying on without pay.

I do strive to be useful. Poor relations must always be useful if they wished to be tolerated.

Emmeline's mood was shifting quickly and she squinted slightly at the brighter light in the kitchen when they climbed from the cellar. Norah saw John noticing it as well. By unspoken mutual agreement, they had Emmeline bundled up and back in John's cart in a matter of minutes. It was a good time to head back to the manor, for the clouds had begun to mask the sun and the afternoon threatened to turn grim.

Vicar Barton kept the pace even on the way back, but he did not pause to point out any more of the village features. Norah rode silently on the other side of Emmeline, her thoughts occupied by light-filled rooms and curved banisters and solid, sandstone walls.

Norah wanted to stay there. She wanted to make tea in the spacious kitchen. She wanted to sit on the deep windowsills and dream.

It was if the house had always been waiting for her—this house that could never be hers.

Even strong wood can break, Miss Grey, if one does not take care.

Should she tell Em about her feelings for John? No. Emmeline might be many things, but Norah did not doubt her loyalty. Em would step aside immediately. Which would do very little to win John for Norah, for he clearly wanted a beautiful bride. If an "Emmeline" was what Vicar John Barton wanted, then a "Norah" would be disqualified before she even began.

Then naive, impulsive Em would still be out in the world, prey to the fortune-hunting jackals of the world. No, if Norah could do nothing else for these two people she loved so much, she could keep their way clear of such confusing side issues.

Her gaze wandered toward the vicar. He sat next to Emmeline, who was now a bit pale and uncharacteristically silent—but of course, still achingly beautiful!—and Norah could not help but see again how astonishing they looked as a couple.

She felt a leaden sadness take her over. Loving Vicar John Barton had changed everything. She'd thought she knew what her future held. She was only now realizing that her destiny was no longer so sure.

I will never be the same after coming to the manor and Haven. I don't think I can ever be satisfied with simply being the dotty auntie to Emmeline's children.

Then she realized something far, far worse.

I cannot live the rest of my days with Emmeline and her husband.

Her husband, John Barton.

The man I love.

The gray wintry day suddenly seemed endless, as if it would last for the rest of her life.

THAT AFTERNOON WHILE Emmeline rested, Norah busied herself

with tying up little portions of sweets in squares of cheerful printed muslin provided by the ever-resourceful Miss Higgins. She used some of Emmeline's extravagant ribbon purchase to make pretty bows, thinking that the girls could keep them as hair ribbons and the boys could give them to their mothers or sisters, although Norah imagined there might be a few ribbon-bedecked puppies running about as well.

The thought made her lips curve in a wistful smile.

Emmeline woke up from her nap much refreshed and ready to dress for the ball. Norah was glad to see it and squelched the tiny voice that said it would have been nice to skip the ball entirely, as a dutiful cousin tending to poor Emmeline. However, Emmeline was getting better every day and an evening of dancing and enjoying herself would do her no harm. Em need not suffer even a jouncing carriage ride home, for the ball would take place only a few floors away from her bedchamber.

Having decided to utilize that very escape plan if she needed it for herself, Norah suddenly felt more able to face the evening's festivities.

Miss Higgins arrived as lady's maid to help Emmeline dress, but Emmeline sweetly insisted that Miss Higgins join them in their preparations. So they were a merry enough trio, oohing and ahhing over Emmeline's dramatic purple silk ball gown strewn with amethyst beads and Norah's simple but luxurious one made of a deep green velvet that threw coppery glints into her tawny hair and, according to Emmeline, her dressmaker and Miss Higgins's experienced eye, made the most of Norah's "assets."

Miss Higgins proudly donned a very pretty woolen gown the exact color of autumnal leaves, trimmed with a twining-vine edging stitched in contrasting yellow-gold embroidery. Emmeline squeaked at the beautiful stitching and dashed for her jewel case. Returning with a choker of golden silk ribbon that held a single carved bit of coral as a centerpiece, she gifted it to Miss Higgins on the spot.

"Norah told me how you nursed me so compassionately while I slept. It is the least I can do to repay you."

"But my lady! It is too fine!"

"I shall never wear it again now," Emmeline said firmly at Miss Higgins's protest. "For it shall always seem lacking without that particular gown to match with it!"

Norah encouraged Miss Higgins as well. "She'll only slip it into your pocket later if you say no. It simply won't do to refuse her."

Miss Higgins bit her lip and accepted the choker, which was very pretty but a mere trinket in comparison to Emmeline's vast collection. It did look divine on Miss Higgins, with her deep brown eyes and her shining dark hair in braids fancifully coiled in high loops.

Emmeline's hairstyle was a complicated arrangement of curled, pinned and artistically loose locks that looked as if they'd tumbled free in effortlessly accidental perfection. Fortunately, it was one of Emmeline's favorite displays, so Norah had a good bit of practice. Miss Higgins thought she might try something similar with her ladyship's hair sometime, though it was "mightily unruly" and would likely "dance right down."

Then Emmeline and Miss Higgins turned on Norah with speculative gazes. "Your turn, miss."

Norah shook her head. "My hair is already done." It was the same as always, her thick braid twisted into a bun and pinned down tight.

Miss Higgins narrowed her eyes. "Not by half, it ain't. I've been itchin' to get me hands on you." She held out one hand to Emmeline. "The pins, my lady? We're going to need all of 'em, me thinks."

"I'm ready." Emmeline gave Norah a cheerfully diabolical grin. "I bought lots of ribbon!"

Chapter 15

J OHN STOOD IN the vast dining room of Havensbeck Manor with most of the village and Matthias, waiting on the arrival of Lady Bernadette and her female guests.

They entered at last in sort of a grand procession. Their fun-loving smiles made it into a celebratory parade instead of a show of wealth and social stature. The inhabitants of Haven seemed very pleased to see "their" ladies put on an impressive spectacle.

To John, all the ladies looked very nice, as if the prospect of dancing gave them an additional shimmer of splendor in expectation. He'd been informed that women went to great lengths to look extra-special for balls, but other than the gowns being a bit richer and hairstyles being a little more elaborate, he'd never really figured out how they went about it.

Then his gaze found Miss Norah Grey and stayed there, riveted. She looked—well, she looked like Norah, only more so. More shine to her hair, more pink to her cheeks, more plumpness to her lips...

And definitely more bosom on display! John froze, half of him lost in dreamy contemplation of such shimmering, ivory-fleshed abundance and the other half of him desiring to stride over there and fling his coat over her shoulders so that no other people—no other men!—could lay eyes upon that lavishness!

Was he being prudish? Looking around her, he could see that several other ladies had necklines just as low, even Lady Blythe and Mrs. Grey.

Yet John felt no compulsion to whisk any of them safely away from view. So it was only Norah. With a firm effort, John reminded himself that he was merely feeling protective of his good friend, who might naively be unaware of the appeal of her generous figure and its impact upon a gentleman's ... ah ... ability to concentrate.

She did look fine, though, didn't she? Her hair seemed different, too, as if she had already danced it into glossy, tumbled disarray. It was piled high and then fell behind her, long and curling halfway down her back. John's hand closed into a gentle fist, recalling the silken texture of her warm, heavy braid in his palm.

As he came closer to the path of the procession that had begun to wind around the dining tables—because he seemed to feel compelled to approach—he saw that although she did seem to have done something to darken her eyebrows and lashes, she still mostly looked like Norah. His Norah, the one that only he had seen: the swift-acting Norah of the bridge rescue, the patient Norah who'd plunked down on the step with little Artie Tanner, and the vulnerable Norah who had shared her sorrowful past in a quiet, fire-lit room.

Most of the crowd seemed especially to enjoy the sight of Lady Emmeline. She was dazzling, of course, in shimmering purple with glimmering jewels.

"Like a princess," someone near John uttered in awe.

"Nay, like a queen!" someone else proclaimed.

John thought Lady Emmeline looked absolutely stunning. Perfect. A budding goddess just stopping by the manor on her rise up to Mount Olympus. So very lovely, really.

Yet his gaze returned to Miss Grey.

She was smiling along with the other ladies, making a playful show with her tasseled silk fan, yet John could tell she was still troubled. The smile didn't quite reach those woods-at-twilight eyes and that gaze that hinted at shadows like wandering mourners amid the trees.

The lord and lady of Havensbeck seated themselves at the high table with their guests. John could likely have qualified to join them but he found he wanted to sit down below with the people of Haven. The fact that it gave him a better view of the ladies did not occur to him at all, not even a little bit.

After the feast, which John was certain was delicious though he hardly recalled what he ate, Lord Matthias and Lady Bernadette rose to give a celebratory Christmas toast and a welcome speech. Soon they would lead the way into the ballroom.

Knowing he had only minutes, John dashed quickly out a side door. He had somewhere to be.

The children of his choir had been left in the ballroom under the dubious supervision of the eldest of them all. It couldn't be helped, for John had not had the heart to ask any Haven adult to miss the dinner which they'd so anticipated. Therefore, there was a bit of hurried clearing up of mischief, wiping of faces and straightening of small cravats and pinafores. Cheerful red woolen scarves were draped across every pair of little shoulders in festive mimicry of the old-fashioned wassail, where a group of singers traveled from door to door in hopes of filling their tankards for a song.

He had just about managed to have the children tidied up and into formation when the large double doors opened and Havensbeck's lord and lady entered at the head of the swarm of guests.

John was so proud of how his previously restless and giggling group suddenly took on a dignified air of attentiveness and looked only at him, their director, instead of gawking at the grand assembly. Well, mostly anyway.

He waited until he knew that the last person had entered and the crowd took on an expectant silence. With his back to his audience, he raised his hands and gave the first motion, a wave to his tiny section of tenors.

"God rest ye, merry gentlemen,
Let nothing you dismay..."

Then he waved the entire choir to join. Their little voices swelled in the large hall. They'd learned how to fill the church with their song and now they projected beautifully in the vast ballroom.

Then it was little Arthur Tanner's turn to step forward and sing. When John saw the child's sickly pallor and wide eyes, he feared the evening might become another mortifying episode for the little chap.

However, Arthur fixed his terrified gaze on something off to one side of John and opened his mouth at the perfect moment. Artie's pure soprano voice rang through the hall like a crystalline chime.

"In Bethlehem, in Israel,
This blessed Babe was born
And laid within a manger
Upon this blessed morn..."

John heard muffled gasps and cries of wonder from the audience and his heart swelled with pride in his choir. As Artie sang on, John cast a glance over his shoulder to see what held the boy's attention so.

It was Miss Grey, standing at the front of the crowd with her gaze fixed on Artie and her lips moving, singing silently along with him.

Artie's solo verse ended and John watched as Miss Grey clapped her hands and bestowed upon Artie a tender smile so full of pride and gentleness that John felt a stab of surprise deep in his chest.

He'd never seen that smile before. It was beautiful, that smile. He found he couldn't look away.

Then he realized that silence had fallen where no silence belonged. He jerked himself back to the present and quickly motioned to the tenors again.

*"Fear not then, said the Angel
Let nothing you affright..."*

AFTER THE PERFORMANCE, Norah watched as Emmeline handed out the little packets of sweets to the brave choral singers. Emmeline knelt right down and congratulated each child in the line, dazzling them one by one. She was so sweet with them that Norah couldn't help but smile.

"You purchased the sweets. Were they not your gift to the children?"

Vicar Barton's deep voice rumbled through Norah and she had to stiffen her knees against a strange tendency to weaken. Without taking her eyes from the choir, Norah answered.

"Yes. But see how delighted Em is? It doesn't matter who gives the gift, does it? The children are happy. Emmeline is happy. I am quite content to make them all happy."

He did not respond but she felt him move closer until his heat warmed the bare skin of her arm. "Again you let Lady Emmeline bask in the attention that you rightfully deserve as well."

"Deserve? What do I deserve, when I am a lodger in my uncle's house at no cost to me? The pennies that bought them came from Emmeline's inheritance, given to me as spending money for the journey. Truly, I do not care if it is Emmeline who is thanked and not I. I did not buy the sweets to garner thanks. I only wished to surprise the children and reward them for their effort. See, they are surprised and rewarded. My wish has been granted." The sensation of warmth grew until the back of her neck felt flushed and fevered.

She wanted to step away from him and his disturbing heat. She wanted to lean into him and be burned to a cinder. Thus conflicted, she remained right where she was, although her thoughts grew less coherent by the moment. She was a tumult of fire and light, ice and darkness, tossed between possible and impossible futures, golden dreams and grim despair.

He is not for me. I cannot have him.

She heard him exhale and felt the warmth of his breath on the side of her neck and across the tops of her breasts.

"Do you never think of yourself, Norah?"

She shook her head quickly. "I am not so virtuous as that, Vicar Barton." She gently rejected his familiar use of her name. "I am as full of bitter unpleasantness as anyone. More perhaps, for I am cursed with a good mind and an excellent imagination. That gives me expansive means to come up with new and exciting ways to be disagreeable, I assure you."

She'd been entirely serious, so no one was more startled than she when he threw back his head and laughed aloud, helplessly and long.

Norah didn't even notice that Emmeline had rejoined her.

ACROSS THE BALLROOM, Bernadette and Simon stood in the reception line with Matthias to greet all their guests one by one.

Simon looked up at John's laugh, then elbowed his sister. "Bernie, did you ever hear John laugh like that? Ever?"

"For pity's sake, Simon, you should eat more. Your elbows are like fireplace pokers!" She paused to look over at John, who stood with Miss Grey, and yes, Lady Emmeline. "He's always been such a serious fellow. Even I never made him laugh like that."

Simon shook his head. "Never ever." He smiled. The second half of his Christmas plan was coming along nicely. He'd saved Christmas by waking the sleeping princess with the promise of Haven's magic. Now he would deliver on that promise with John Barton on a silver platter.

John would never have to drink his own bad tea again.

"DID YOU SEE their little faces shine? Aren't they adorable?" Lady Emmeline seemed so ecstatic over the reception given the sweets that John didn't have the heart to resent her for stealing Miss Grey's thunder. Miss Grey seemed quite correct that Lady Emmeline meant no harm by it and was all eagerness to share her plenty.

Her timing, however, could be better. John had just caught his breath when Lady Emmeline popped up at his elbow. He'd not had time to ask Miss Grey for the first waltz.

"Oh listen! The quartet is playing a waltz!" Lady Emmeline turned a melting gaze upon John.

There was no help for it. Miss Grey was already moving away, seeming terribly interested in the refreshment tables. John repressed a sigh and smiled down at Lady Emmeline. "My lady, dare I beg a dance?"

Of course, she was a perfect dancer. Knowing what Miss Grey had described to him, John pictured hours of ferocious training by a dancing master who had found a naturally graceful pupil. He certainly knew all about that situation.

He endeavored to live up to his own master's teachings and soon they were sweeping grandly about the floor whilst the other dancers stood back to watch. It was enjoyable to dance a proper waltz again. He'd always felt constrained by his station, for it would not do to mislead some fervent village miss when he held such a position of responsibility in the community. Country dances were fine, in square or lines of dancers. The waltz, however, was for couples.

Oh no. Lady Emmeline was doing it again, shining her large, mesmerizing eyes at him and focusing every fiber of her being at convincing him that he was the man of her dreams.

He felt like pulling a face, or making a joke, or intentionally stepping on her toes, anything to break the hunting-cat intensity of her gaze. It felt—insincere, if he dared think such a thing of a respectable lady.

When in doubt, John usually reverted to honesty. "Lady Emmeline, I am feeling rather uncomfortable. Would you mind not looking at me in that way?"

She blinked in surprise and the pressure eased. "In what way, Vicar Barton?"

He could pretend to have been mistaken. He could change the subject, talk about the village, or compliment her gown. Instead, he followed an impulse inspired by Miss Grey. "You don't need to do that, my lady. You are a stunning beauty and a gracious, sweet-natured lady. Every man you meet likely already thinks you are irresistible. There's no need to ... ahem ... cast a spell."

To his surprise, she made no pretense of not knowing of what he spoke. "Truly? You don't think I need to fascinate you with my eyes?"

John barked a small, relieved laugh. "You truly don't, trust me. Your eyes are exceptionally fascinating, all on their own."

"All right then."

For some moments, they merely danced. John was just beginning to regain his earlier enjoyment when she spoke again. "What of my opinions? Do you believe I must conceal my true opinions for fear that men will be put off?"

John was beginning to recognize Miss Grey's subversive ideas had clearly taken root behind Lady Emmeline's pretense of demure feminine submission. He felt it was the least he could do to support that influence.

"My lady, no man with any character could possibly object to a refined lady's considered and thoughtful opinions." He thought of his mother, a faded shadow of his father. "Or even her ill-considered and spontaneous opinions, for that matter. After all, men do not restrain theirs, among their equals."

She seemed lost in thought for a moment as they continued to whirl in perfect graceful unison. The music ended and they came smoothly to a stop.

Then, she tilted her head and gave him a mischievous, gamine's smile. It was breathtaking, actually. Far more riveting than all her other practiced expressions.

"Then, Vicar Barton, I am of the *opinion* that we should keep dancing."

He smiled and bowed. "Then this rousing country dance is all yours, my lady."

Chapter 16

E MMELINE AND VICAR Barton were dancing again. Emmeline seemed to float in a bubble of delight and the vicar looked well pleased with himself.

Norah tried very hard not to die from the ache behind her breastbone. John would be so very good to Emmeline. Norah would never have to worry that her sweet, heedless cousin would ever be repressed or abused. John would look after Emmeline. His kindly nature would support her and his sensible attitudes would keep her safe.

No cruel governess would dare trespass on John Barton's watch, that was for certain!

Norah searched her soul for gratitude. Emmeline had not died. Emmeline had found an excellent match, one that would both please her father and also ensure that she would be cherished forever and always.

It was all she'd ever wanted for Emmeline.

She closed her eyes. "I am grateful. I am grateful."

"Of course you are, Miss Grey! We all are! 'Tis a wondrous evening, is it not?"

Norah opened her eyes to find Mr. Jasper before her, his eyes bright and his cheeks a smidge more flushed than they ought to be. Mr. Jasper had been at Mrs. Vicar's "fortifying" sherry, she would wager. And if she was not mistaken, that was a sprig of mistletoe he wore pinned to his lapel.

Cheeky fellow! She had to smile back at his sozzled grin. "It is indeed a splendid party, Mr. Jasper."

"Yet you are not dancing, Miss Grey. You must dance. If you do not, I shall put pepper in your biscuits. I have it on good authority that it is a most persuasive means of ... um." He blinked hard at her for a moment. "Of persuasion! Come, won't you dance?"

Norah looked up to see that the dance forming was a quick-stepping formation of hooked elbows and ducking beneath arched arms. It seemed familiar enough to her. Further, she was heartily sick of her own doldrums.

She packed a bit of cotton wool around her cracked heart and put it carefully away for later consideration, preferably at a time when she was not standing in the middle of a grand, giddy Christmas celebration.

Ducking a quick curtsy, she beamed at Mr. Jasper. "Why thank you, sir! I should love to take a turn about the floor!"

It was a familiar dance, but committed at a break-neck speed. She was gasping and laughing by the end. Suddenly, young Mr. Tanner, the footman, was at her elbow. Behind him, she saw several local fellows who had been headed her way now grimacing in apparent disappointment that Mr. Tanner had beaten them to her side.

Goodness. They want to dance ... with me?

At the Society balls she'd attended with Emmeline, the few times she'd been asked to dance was when some enterprising suitor had pressed Norah to advance his pursuit of Lady Emmeline.

It was an interesting sensation, being sought after. It was likely due more to her adventure on the bridge than her actual appeal, but at least the admiration was sincere. Furthermore, she was certain her hair had never looked so good.

It is amusing to overdo once in a while, don't you find?

"Why yes, Mr. Tanner. I should very much like to dance!"

JOHN WATCHED NORAH dancing with Billy Tanner.

Lady Emmeline had been snatched away for a dance by Lord Matthias and then by Lord Bester, so John had ducked off for a bit of cake and a glass of champagne. That the refreshment table had an excellent view of the dance floor was mere coincidence.

Though Norah seemed more mature of the two, John realized suddenly that she and Billy Tanner were of an age.

In the beautiful gown that brought out the color of her eyes, with her artistically tumbled hair looking quite stylish, not to mention the accentuation of assets naturally bequeathed by nature, John thought Norah looked very ... um, delightful. Surely he shouldn't be surprised that other young men thought so too.

It was her smile, he decided. She was smiling. A lot. In fact, she was smiling at every dewy, baby-faced fellow who asked her gallop about the floor with them.

The only person she had not smiled at all evening—and he had kept count!—was him, her friend, Vicar John Barton of Haven in Staffordshire!

John plunked his plate of untasted cake down onto a table and tossed back his full flute of champagne. He might not have earned a smile yet, but by gum, he meant to win one!

THE PREVIOUS SET ended with cherub-cheeked Mr. Brand spinning Norah from the circle dance until she couldn't stand. She found herself leaning dizzily on the young man's arm, laughing at him as he playfully smirked at her.

"Aye, yer a fine dancer, miss! Would ye—"

"I believe the lady would like to catch her breath."

Norah looked up to see Vicar Barton smiling benignly down at her. His expression when he turned to Mr. Brand was somewhat less benevolent. Brand's carefree smile faded.

"Hello, Vicar. Er ... Happy Christmas?"

"Mr. Brand, I think your mother would send you to the kitchens for something substantial to eat. And perhaps a bit of strong tea."

Brand blinked. "Did I overstep, sir?"

Vicar Barton smiled with a few too many teeth. "Not yet."

Norah had caught her breath by then, but Brand had already disappeared in a wave of the vicar's judgmental hand. Norah rolled her eyes. "That was entirely unnecessary. Mr. Brand is a just a child."

The vicar took her elbow and steered her to the edge of the floor, out of the way of the next couples. "Mr. Brand is old enough to drink champagne and dance with young ladies, Miss Grey. Did you have very much champagne?"

That startled her. She straightened and turned on him with snapping eyes. "I haven't had a drop, sir!"

He tilted his head at her. "You are having a very good time, Miss Grey. Perhaps I misspoke, but I have never seen you so ... so abandoned."

"Ah, I see. You believe that I am neglecting my chaperoning

duties! With my mother and my great-aunt in the ballroom? Why shouldn't I? I am as young and unwed as Emmeline, you recall. Perhaps someone should be chaperoning me!"

He gazed down at her for a long moment. "I have further offended you, Miss Grey. I wish I knew what I am doing wrong that you cannot abide me. Again."

He bobbed a curt bow and began to turn away. Then he turned back. "No. I came to you to try to comprehend. I mean to understand." He held out his hand. "Will you grant me this dance, Miss Grey?"

It was so directly a scene from her deepest dreams that Norah put her hand in his before she absorbed the fact that the quartet had begun another waltz tune. White-hot shock moved through her as he took her into his arms.

She knew she was a good dancer. Emmeline had trained with a professional and Norah had been her practice partner. Other than a tendency to forget the lady's part and try to lead, she was every bit as good a dancer as Emmeline, if a tad less elegant in form.

Just once. Just this one dance with him. A single, perfect heartbreaking moment to carry with her into her misty, uncertain future.

He swept her into the dance and she lifted her chin and waltzed with the man she loved.

"I love you. I know you love Emmeline, but I love you with everything I am. I just wanted you to know."

Of course, she didn't say the words aloud.

DANCING WITH NORAH was different than dancing with Emmeline. The waltz with Lady Emmeline had been a display, a performance by two carefully trained show ponies, a matched pair of check-reined carriage horses, sculpted and curried by two sets of parents to bring honor to their families and continue the line, breeding like to like. John had enjoyed the excellence of the dance itself, but he knew perfectly well that it had meant nothing special to either of them.

Dancing with Norah made him *aware*.

Of her. Of himself. Of the pounding of his own pulse.

The other dancers faded away. Even the music was only a distant guide to their steps. He felt everything, the warm velvet of her gown against his wrist, the sweep of her skirts as they clung to his legs when he spun her. The lightness in her step when she spun back into his arms. She moved with a sensual depth that light-footed Emmeline had not. Her body fitted close to his with a sense of familiarity. The scent of her teased at his senses to remind him of vanilla and cinnamon and sweet, woodland air.

He wanted the tune to go on longer, but it ended all too soon. His fingers wanted to cling to hers when he released her hand and stepped back to bow. She curtsied, just as expected, but when she straightened, her gaze locked with his for a long, fraught moment.

He froze, gazing down deep into a secret forest, complicated and mysterious, shadowed with dusk.

Then she was gone, slipping away between the new couples advancing onto the floor.

John felt as though someone had kicked him in the belly. What he had seen, what she had allowed him to see, whether she meant to or not—

God help me. Norah had feelings for him. Strong feelings.

Oh no. It was a mistake, a terrible error. It was something that should never have happened.

He'd been careless, so thoughtless. In his loneliness, he'd longed for a friend. When he'd met caustic, clever Norah Grey, he'd begun to seek out her company, simply for the unusual opportunity to clash wits with an equal mind.

Yet that dark, seething look of longing she'd let him see? And something else, as well. He'd perceived a deep and terrible injury in her dark eyes and he had the alarming feeling that he'd dealt her that wound.

He'd been so unfair to her. So selfish to pursue their friendship simply to ease his own isolation. There was practically an entire year at seminary school devoted to the dire consequences of accidentally encouraging familiar behavior with female parishioners, for heaven's sake!

He should stop if Norah was becoming confused. He would stop, at once. God, yes, he'd stop! She'd been right to treat him distantly and he would respect that. He would do the same.

I don't want to stop.

Being lonely was no excuse. His own needs didn't matter. His primary concern should be to help Miss Norah Grey by keeping his distance.

But I really, truly don't want to stop. I don't want to be with her less. I want to be with her more.

I want to be with her all the time.

That realization shook him to the core.

"OH, NOTTIE!" EMMELINE wailed. "Oh my head!"

Norah took her limp, overtired cousin into her arms like she would comfort a child. "I know, pet. I know. It's been a lovely night, but it's time for you to rest somewhere dark and quiet, isn't it?"

Emmeline sniffled. "Dark! Oh, yes, the candles are like daggers, Nottie!"

Norah looked around for Miss Higgins. She finally spotted the maid half-hidden behind a potted palm. With, ahem, Mr. Tanner. *Oh my goodness.*

She turned Emmeline aside. "Let's let Miss Higgins enjoy the ball, Em. I have you, pet. We'll take you right upstairs and then I'll fetch you a cup of weak tea and a bit of toast. Did you have very much champagne, Emmie?"

"No. Perhaps. I don't recall. I danced and danced! Oh, Nottie, country balls are ever so much more fun than Society balls. No one counted my waltzes or made me sit out every third dance or made me drink that awful warm lemonade like at Almack's." She leaned heavily on Norah and staggered a little. "Oh my head," she whispered. "Shhh..."

Lady Bernadette came out of nowhere and took Emmeline's other arm. "Here we go, Lady Emmeline. Just a few stairs ahead." She glanced at Norah as they headed for the door. "And what about you, Miss Grey? Have you had enough merry-making, or would you like to return to the ball?"

Norah shook her head quickly. She'd very nearly spilled her broken heart out at Vicar Barton's feet like a tray of broken china so that he dare not take a step until Jasper had someone sweep her up and put her into the dustbin. There was no telling what she might do if she returned to the ball.

No, she had danced her dance. It was time she saw to picking up her broken bits and mending them as best she could.

JOHN WATCHED NORAH, Emmeline and Bernadette leave the ballroom. Even after they were out of sight, he continued to gaze thoughtfully at the doorway.

"Something on your mind, Vicar?"

John looked hard at Matthias. Here might be someone who knew a thing or two about the world shifting sideways on a man when a woman looked at him a certain way.

"How did you know you wanted to marry her?"

After a reflective moment, Matthias tilted his head. "I was going to ask you which time. Then I realized it doesn't matter. It's comfortably cut and dried, John. Ask yourself one question." Matthias looked up into the glitter of the chandelier above them. "How do you feel about waking up next to her for the rest of your life?"

John felt that jolt again, that shock like ice water, only warmer and more wonderful. "I'd actually hate to contemplate the alternative, if I'm honest."

"Hmm." Matthias rocked back on his heels a few times. "Well, well. You know, I could have a word with Lord Bester on your behalf, if you'd like."

John, who had lost the thread a bit while contemplating waking up next to Norah, all sleepy eyes and tumbled hair and warm, welcoming softness, only mumbled an absentminded "Thank you, my lord."

Chapter 17

RISING EARLY ON Christmas Day, John left the manor and walked through a silent, silvery morning into Haven. He lead a quiet little service in the church that was, unsurprisingly, very poorly attended indeed. No matter. When the ball's survivors had rested and fed and nursed their aching heads into the afternoon, John meant to do it all again at sundown.

After he made his farewells to the five elderly folk who had faced down the icy morning, John made a stop at the vicarage.

For two days, John had been trying to come up with a gift for Norah. It had not been until last night that he'd realized the obvious.

He had found items among his belongings for everyone else in the family. On the dining table before him lay a heavy, gilt-trimmed book on the Battle of Hastings for Lord Bester. He had chosen a silver page marker for Lady Blythe and a Chinese silk one for Mrs. Grey. People always seemed to think a man who carried a bible needed more page markers!

He was quite enthusiastic over his gift for Matthias, oddly enough. Even at the worst of his misery, he'd known that the gold Roman coin he'd found when digging his new cistern was meant for the Lord of Havensbeck.

Possibly because it did, technically belong to him. If anything, John's "gift" consisted of unearthing, carefully polishing and finding a small velvet bag to present his lordship's own coin to him.

For Simon, John had one of his old lead soldiers. It had been his favorite as a boy and it was one of the few things he'd taken from his home when he became a man. It was a cavalry officer on a long-legged horse. The paint was chipped but still bright. John thought Simon would enjoy it.

Lady Bernadette would receive one of the cuttings from the rose bush in front of the vicarage, which she had admired. Since John had brought the original from the gardens of the Bishop's Palace at

Gloucester, the rose did not actually belong to Matthias. John had started many cuttings but only two had survived. The other he meant to give to Sarah Goodrich, who had cared for him more than his own mother had while he'd studied with the vicar.

For the vicar, he had a letter. There was never a man less interested in material possessions than Vicar Goodrich, so John had written down for the vicar his gratitude for being shown another way, a better way, to serve.

He had two other gifts in his pocket. A lady's lapel pin, the sort of thing worn on a riding habit, figured of a gold fox with an amethyst eye. It was a simple thing he'd purchased on his travels because the expressive little fox amused him. This was clearly destined to belong to Lady Emmeline.

He only had one thing of much value left. He didn't take it out to put with the others, for it was nothing like them. Simply holding it in his hand caused a curious exhilaration in his soul. And yes, a little bit of panic as well.

"NOTTIE, LOOK! IT'S starting to snow! Goodness, Staffordshire has much more snow than London, or the Abbey." Emmeline sighed and pressed her nose to the window glass like a child. "It is pretty but so cold! I shouldn't like to see it every Christmas morning, would you?"

Norah took another sip of her tea and gave an noncommittal "Mmm."

As a matter of fact, I would, if it wouldn't remind me of painful things.

They were having a late breakfast in Emmeline's sitting room. Norah was dressed but Emmeline still felt a bit unsteady and was resisting dressing at all. Wrapped in her heavy velvet dressing gown, she sat by the window with her feet curled beneath her and gazed at the falling whiteness.

"Do you think it is snowing everywhere as it is here?"

Norah moved to stand behind Em and stroked a gentle hand over her forehead. "No pet. I daresay it is raining in London. How is your headache? Better?"

Emmeline cast Norah a fondly irritated glare over her shoulder. "If someone asks me that just once more, I believe I shall scream."

Norah laughed ruefully. "Don't do that. I'm much too sore from dancing to sit on you right now." She stretched her arms over her head. "I don't think I've ever danced so much, not even if you put every ball and assembly together in one evening!"

Emmeline leaned her forehead against the cold glass and smiled as she closed her eyes. "It was marvelous, wasn't it? We shall come back every year, I think. After all, we are part of the family!" She sighed. "John is such a wonderful dancer. Imagine how fine he will look in proper evening silks!"

Norah honestly could not imagine a man like John in silks. A man who remade his house and dug terrace stones with his own hands? Oh, those hands.

Norah hid her disquiet by pouring herself another cup of tea, though she didn't want it. The family was about to grow, wasn't it?

Cousin John. Even trying it out in the privacy of her own mind made Norah's belly flip unpleasantly. If Emmeline was as a sister to her, then John Barton must become as a brother. That simple fact would burden Norah with a shocking secret. She wasn't sure she could bear up under it, she who had always endeavored to be honest, even if she could not manage to be truly good.

Therefore, she feared she must leave the Abbey and Emmeline behind her, her uncle and great-aunt and even Mama as well. Poor Mama would be too terrified to leave Lady Blythe and her precious security behind to accompany Norah into the world.

Did love always ruin lives as hers was to be ruined? That would make picturesque little Haven—charming, magical Haven!—into a cursed place, not a blessed one!

She covered her face with her hands, knowing that Emmeline was too immersed in her own sickly feelings to notice Norah's. I have been so unwise, and now I should accept that I must pay. Yet an old anger did twist within her, that lifelong sense of injustice that although she had done nothing wrong, she had been born unbeautiful ... and look what it had cost her!

Such unworthy thoughts on a sacred day! She shook herself out of her selfish stew and took a breath. If she were to lose her family soon, then she ought not to waste this last, lovely Christmas on dreading the future.

She turned to Emmeline with a smile. "I have a gift for you!"

It was a dainty pair of earbobs of opal and gold. Norah had inherited them from her and Emmeline's grandmother, the sister of Great-Aunt Blythe, and Norah knew Emmeline had always admired them.

"Really? For me!" Emmeline squealed like a little girl being gifted a new doll and scrambled out of the window seat. She ran to kiss Norah on the cheek. "I don't see how you can bear to part with them!" Taking the little silk case, Emmeline danced to the dressing table to put them on her earlobes. Then she whirled to face Norah. "What do you think?"

Norah shook her head. "I think you shall start a new fashion of opals and dressing gowns, you lazy moppet. Why don't you get dressed now?"

"Oh, but I have a gift for you, too!"

Norah blinked. Gift-giving, at least the non-spontaneous kind, wasn't one of Emmeline's strong suits. Planning ahead to bring a gift along on their journey was practically unheard of!

It was a soft thing wrapped in pretty tissue. Norah opened it to find a lovely silk reticule of green and cream, embroidered all over with charming little flowers. "Because you love the garden at the Abbey," Emmeline chirped. "See, I've done the daisy and the columbine and the peony—"

Norah stared at her cousin. "You made this? For me?"

Emmeline grinned. "Oh, it's been such a trial! I cannot tell you how many times you almost caught me with my needle! Once I had to stuff it in my bodice, you ran into the library so fast!"

Norah bit her lip and stroked the lovely thing. "I cannot believe you made this for me. It is so much work!"

Emmeline wrinkled her nose. "Well, it was supposed to be for your sixteenth birthday, so you can see I was not diligent at all."

Norah laughed. Even while the tears of broken-heartedness and loss streamed down her face, she laughed so hard she got the hiccups. When she caught her breath and wiped her eyes, she gazed at silly, sweet, perfectly beautiful Emmeline without remembering to be envious for once in her life. "Promise me that I will never lose you, Emmie. No matter where the world takes us, promise me that we shall always be so close as we are now."

Emmeline leaped into Norah's arms and hugged her more tightly than one might expect of such a delicate beauty. "Don't worry, Nottie. We shall be together forever!"

WHEN NORAH AND Emmeline joined the family downstairs, it was for a lazy luncheon, picked from a serving table and consumed casually without wait-staff.

"I've given most everyone the day to rest and see their families," Lady Bernadette told them. "Only Cook wouldn't budge, so we shall at least eat."

No one had much appetite but young Simon, who went back to the serving table twice for more cold ham. "When is John coming back? He said he had a surprise for me."

Norah realized that she and Emmeline did not have a gift for John Barton. They'd known enough about the Havensbeck family to have chosen a few things like a silver hairbrush set for Lady Bernadette and a set of jet-buttoned cuff-chains for Lord Matthias. For Simon, Norah had steered Emmeline away from a pretty miniature china tea set toward a book on snakes and lizards, with detailed illustrations of the consumption of frogs that made Emmeline pull a face. "Really?"

"Oh yes," Norah answered. She had sometimes played with the commoner children who lived around the Abbey—something Emmeline had never been allowed to do—so she spoke from experience. "Boys adore snakes." Personally, she thought snakes were all right, as long as they stayed on the pages of the book.

Uncle Bester also gained an ostentatious set of cuff-chains and Mama and Great-Aunt Blythe received very pretty page markers. Emmeline had paid for everything, of course, but since Norah had helped her choose wisely, Emmeline insisted that the gifts were from both of them. Yet they had nothing for the surprise family friend, Vicar John Barton.

Swiftly, Norah ran up to her chamber, to a little escritoire in the corner. It was left fully supplied for guests. Soon she was scratching away, unaware that she wrote with a sad little smile on her face.

WHEN JOHN ARRIVED at the manor, energized by the weather and just a little numbed in the extremities, the cheerful parlor full of

Greys and Goodriches and Havensbeck occupants felt like stepping into his own home. Better, for he was met with cries of welcome and smiles beamed from every point in the room.

It was great fun handing out his gifts. Simon was giddy over the soldier and Bernadette immediately rushed off to water the little cutting. Matthias seemed very impressed by the coin and suggested that they tear down the vicarage to look for more.

His lordship certainly had a strange sense of humor.

Lord Bester's eyes lit up at the great thumping history book. Lady Blythe and Mrs. Grey exclaimed that they truly needed page markers and wasn't he a thoughtful lad?

Sarah Goodrich also fled the room to water her little rose, leading John to suspect he'd been doing it wrong. Vicar Goodrich read his letter silently and then carefully folded it up, placing it into his breast pocket over his heart. He didn't say a word, but when he tilted his head to look up at John, there was a suspicious shine in his mentor's eyes.

Then Lady Emmeline handed John a letter of his own.

He opened it to read aloud, "A Pamphlet on the Preparation of Parsnips."

John laughed until his belly ached. As he wiped at his streaming eyes, he saw Bernadette reenter the room and cast a knowing look at Matthias. That was when John noticed that everyone seemed to be staring at him. He felt a sudden urge to surreptitiously check that his trouser buttons were completely fastened.

Not knowing what else to do, he remained very still and tried not to fidget. "Ah, is there something I ought to know?"

"Ha!" Lord Bester shouted it more than laughed it. He shook a finger at John and approached him with his beefy hand stuck out. "My boy!"

John blinked and allowed Lord Bester to pump his hand. Oh no. He had a sudden recollection of Matthias saying he would speak to Bester...

Well, this was regrettably public but that didn't really matter, did it? "I'd meant to speak to you privately, my lord—"

"Privately! Ha!" Bester clapped him on the back so hard that John would have staggered were he not a head taller than the older man. "Oh you're a sly one, Barton!"

John blinked. "No, I'm truly not." This wasn't right. He needed to speak to Norah.

He looked around for her, but all he saw was Lady Emmeline, who suddenly looked rather sickly and wide-eyed. Then he saw gray skirts swish away through the parlor door. Norah? "Wait—"

"Emmeline, come on, no need to be shy!" Lady Blythe towed Lady Emmeline closer, followed by Mrs. Grey, her face wreathed in smiles.

"Wait, but I—" John felt as if he'd gone a little mad. Nothing was making sense. He looked down at Lady Emmeline, hoping she would say something, anything to stop what was happening. Her gaze was fixed blindly on a far wall, as if she couldn't bear to look at him.

Then it hit him that it might already be too late. Somehow, the entire family had formed the impression that John had been courting Lady Emmeline! That was absurd! Yes, he'd once brought her a plate of food and he'd taken her for a drive and then he'd danced with her a few times—well, rather a lot perhaps—but it was just a family party, so dancing didn't mean—

If he felt numb and horrified, it was nothing to Lady Emmeline's condition. She reeled slightly on her feet, as if she felt blown over by her father's blustery plans. Clearly, for all her flirtatious ways, she had no real desire to wed him either!

John's thoughts sped like a panicked horse. *I have to stop this. If someone actually utters the word "engagement" it will ruin everything!*

Once it had been uttered out loud, John could not refute an engagement, not without besmirching Lady Emmeline's reputation and absolutely scourging his own name. He'd lose his position as well, for the Church wanted no such untrustworthy servants!

Releasing Bernadette to wed the man she loved was one thing. The engagement had never left the family and had been dissolved in the course of a single morning. But to refute Lady Emmeline when her father clearly wanted the match and then to propose to her cousin? At the Greys' level of society, the gossip would storm for years!

He would have to see it through. Lady Emmeline would have to see it through. They would be forced to marry.

Then a new and more terrible panic seized him.

Oh heavens, what must Norah think? She'd fled the room, she must have been under the same impression—

Norah!

Then it happened. Mrs. Grey clapped her hands, her expression rapturous. "Isn't it romantic!"

No, please, no don't say it!

Mrs. Grey smiled at them all. "A Christmas enga—"

"*Emmeline!*"

Chapter 18

*E*MMELINE!"

John started at the boyish bellow coming from outside the parlor, but his reaction was nothing compared to Lady Emmeline's.

She came to life like a doll magically transformed into a real live girl. "Bertie? *Bertie!*"

A tall, slight man burst into the parlor. He looked as though he'd ridden in the snow for hours, for it crusted on his shoulders and he carried a thick layer on the top of his hat.

Jasper had the day off, John thought inanely. The fellow simply walked in.

Someone had said the word. Hadn't they? He felt breathless and icy inside. Did it count? Was he engaged to the wrong woman? Had he just lost every chance of true happiness?

"Emmeline!" The desperate fellow threw himself at Lady Emmeline so forcefully that John thought, just an instant too late, that he ought to step between them.

It wouldn't have worked anyway, for Emmeline was flinging herself at "Bertie" with equal force. "Oh, my angel!"

The two collided in front of the fireplace, knocking chunks of snow from the man's clothing into the coals to sizzle fiercely there as they practically devoured each other in a passionate kiss.

Matthias stood next to John. "Sorry, Vicar. Foiled again."

JOHN STOMPED ALONG the lane. He'd searched the snow-covered estate for Norah for half an hour to no avail. If she'd gone into the village, he might still spot her tracks in the fresh snow, though more was coming down.

Then she was there, just ahead of him. She stood on the bridge, not too close to the wall, and gazed out at the frozen river. John halted and took a deep breath of relief.

He'd found her.

Yes. At last, I have found her.

There, in her grey cloak with the snow collecting on its deep hood, stood the most wonderful woman John had ever met.

It was not just physical attraction, although he was attracted. Very.

What he saw in Norah was something he'd been promised in his study of the Book. It was a holy gift. It was a meeting of minds and a shared humor. It came beautifully accompanied by a forthright heart and a bright soul unsullied by superficial concerns.

He considered all the generous, astonishing things he'd seen her do, large and small, recognized and unrecognized.

Oh Miss Norah Grey, your potential is squandered as simply your cousin's companion. What may I offer you instead? Myself? My children? My flock?

What might your unstinting heart accomplish with an entire village under your wing?

He rather thought she might enjoy finding out. He knew he would.

VICAR BARTON APPROACHED her slowly. Norah didn't look at him yet. If she didn't look, he wouldn't speak. If he didn't speak, he wouldn't inform her of his happy news and then she would not have to congratulate him on his good fortune.

Just one minute more, please. One minute, out in the snow again with the man I love.

Before he becomes someone I may only esteem.

"I would think you'd prefer to avoid this spot."

"Do you know, I think it is now my favorite place in the world." She heard the wistful sadness revealed in her voice, but she had not the will to lie just yet.

He scuffled to a stop near her. Norah flinched away, turning to walk quickly toward the village. As quickly as she could, at any rate, with the fresh snow risen above her ankles.

Vicar Barton ran to match stride with her. With his hands stuck deep into his pockets and his head down, he made Norah think of a boy who didn't want to go to school.

"Do you know, the strangest thing just happened."

Norah didn't speak. *Don't answer. Just one more minute.*

"That Bertie fellow—is he entirely mad, or simply mad about Lady Emmeline?"

Norah stopped short. Of all the things she'd expected...

Blast the man! She had to ask. "What does Lord Bertram have to do with anything?"

"Well, considering that right now Lady Blythe, Lady Bernadette and your mother are all planning the wedding of the century—"

Norah died a little more.

"And Lady Emmeline can't stop kissing the poor sod long enough for him to come up for air—"

"What?" She whirled on him, her mouth agape.

He was grinning underneath his hat, the arse!

Then he started to laugh. "It's true! I know, I thought I was about to become engaged as well! But then Lord Bertram Ardmore broke down the door, all covered in snow. I am not, in fact, Lady Emmeline's 'angel.' It was all allegedly very amusing, except I was mostly just baffled."

He wasn't going to marry Emmeline. He was free!

And then it struck her. It didn't matter that he was free, because men like John Barton didn't fall in love with women like Norah Grey. They fell in love with women like Emmeline.

Only then, she was ashamed to admit, did it occur to Norah that John had suffered a terrible loss. Aching for him, she put a hand on his arm. "So again, the woman you'd meant to marry has fallen in love with someone else?"

"Actually, I think she was always in love with him. It was all quite garbled, you understand, but apparently when she inherited, she was surrounded by new suitors. Bertie had his feelings injured when she began favoring one of them."

"Oh, Emmeline," Norah sighed. "It was a tactic," she explained to John. "She was trying to get Lord Bertram to declare for her by making him jealous."

"Oh, kick him to the starting line, so to speak?" John nodded thoughtfully. "Well, he went away thinking she didn't care for him."

"Ah. And then when he heard of Emmeline's accident?"

"Oh yes. Rode for days, although he made it sound like weeks, but that would start him in Spain, so I don't know—"

To her surprise, Norah laughed aloud. John smiled at her.

In fact, he truly *smiled* at her. Her heart started to pound. She swallowed hard. "So you aren't engaged to Emmeline, but Lord Bertram is?"

"You might think I would become accustomed to losing out to other gentlemen. It seems to be my fate."

Norah hesitated. "Are you ... very heartbroken?"

He looked up, down the winding lane and the snow-laden branches lining it. "Actually, my overwhelming reaction was utter and total relief."

"What? Why?" She suddenly felt contrarily defensive of Emmeline. "What's so wrong with Emmeline?"

He shrugged. "Oh nothing. Nothing at all. She's beautiful, charming, good-natured, rich..."

Norah was feeling a little worse at that point.

"However, Lady Emmeline Grey bears one unredeemable flaw. One which I fear I could never tolerate."

"What is it?" He was going to say Em wasn't terribly bright. It was somewhat true, but Norah couldn't bear for anyone to mock sweet Emmeline. She truly couldn't endure to hear John be so unkind.

He turned to smiled down at her. "She isn't you."

What? "No. Don't mock me like that. Everyone—*everyone*— prefers Emmeline!"

He shook his head slowly back and forth, his pewter gaze never leaving hers. "Not everyone."

She couldn't allow herself to believe it. She backed away, one hand out in protest. "No. You don't really know me. I'm too—too— bookish! Outspoken! Cynical!"

He caught her hand and followed her retreat. "Too intelligent. Too honest. Too clear-sighted. Too kind."

"Oh no." She shook her head wildly, knocking her hood from her head. "I'm not that kind. Not in my mind. I think terrible things about people, about how weak they are, or afraid, or appalling." *I'm the appalling one!* "I'm very bad at being good!"

He wrapped her in his arms. "It isn't unkind to simply comprehend the weakness and flaws in people. It could be used as a gift—one that allows you to help them shore up their cracked foundations and build better character upon them."

It sounded like an impossible task. "That must be a terrible burden to carry! How do you do it?"

He leaned back to laugh at her. "I was hoping you'd tell me!" He began to draw her closer. "You let Emmeline give the gifts, because someday it might teach her to be more thoughtful. You saw the grief in a boy who I thought was merely nervous. You found a way to teach a blundering bachelor how to keep his secret from his housekeeper and eat his parsnips, too."

He spoke with such admiration in his voice. About her?

She almost fell under his spell, then she pushed him away. "I'm never going to be an Emmeline. Or a Bernadette. I'm not likely to get any prettier, you know."

He leaned back and ran appreciative eyes over her face and form. "Heaven forbid! I doubt my heart could stand it!" The flare of heat in his eyes turned them dark and a little hungry.

She shivered. A very nice sort of shiver.

Then it was too late to stop him. He went down on one knee and reached into his coat to his weskit pocket and withdrew something. Norah stared down at his open palm. There lay a dainty gold ring, set with a small pearl.

"I'm an oyster," she breathed. Somehow, it was better than being compared to a flower, or a gazelle, or a goddess, as men had been wont to do to Emmeline. It wasn't empty, obvious flattery.

It was a title given by someone who had actually looked inside to see her as she truly was.

"It belonged to my mother's mother," he said. "I remember that she loved me very much, though I lost her when I was only a child. I've just realized why I've been thinking of her so much lately." He smiled up at her. "I have such fond memories of her laughter."

Strangely, Norah had begun to believe.

He went on. "I should speak to your uncle first, I suppose, although that always seems rather like a horse deal to me—"

If it was at all possible, she might've fallen a little more deeply in love with him at that moment.

"—But I want to ask you and I want to hear your answer—"

"Yes." It wasn't a hard question.

He ignored her. "Miss Norah Grey, will you—"

"Yes."

He pressed his lips together tightly, but she saw the corners twitch anyway. He began again. "Will you do me the great honor of—"

"Y—" His glare of exasperation over his huge grin stopped her. No one had ever looked at her with such—

Clarity.

Understanding.

Love. For her, just as she was, without reservation.

He truly sees me.

Suddenly, she wanted to hear it. She wanted the whole proposal, the entire silly romantic moment, the declaration of his feelings, the question. "Start over."

He looked up at her with raised brows.

She smiled shyly. "Please? I won't say a word, a promise. But just in case you're wondering, I'm going to say—"

"*MISS NORAH GREY,*" he bellowed. "I love you! I want to marry you! I want to have six or seven little Norahs arguing around the dinner table every evening!"

Oh heavens. That was rather a lot. She didn't say a word, but she could feel her smile stretch into a grin. Smart outspoken daughters. What fun!

"I want to grow old with you and help you out of your rocker every night and wake up next to you every morning!"

Cheeky sod. I'll be the one hefting you up, just you wait! Her heart was singing.

"This isn't going at all well but that's fine because I think I know your answer." He took a breath at last and waited, smiling up at her confidently.

She couldn't resist. "I ... may I think about it? Just for a few days. A month, just a few months. You know, I'm sure I'll come to an answer by summer—"

With a growl he rose to his feet, taking her with him. His strong arms wrapped around her hips... and his hands gripped her bottom. Oh my goodness. Her mind went blank with the fizzing of her senses. "What ... what were we talking about?"

He started to laugh. He laughed so hard he fell back into a snow bank, pulling her down on top of him as he roared.

It was likely a bit naughty to want to stay right where she was. Or even to think about wriggling a bit.

Oh, yes. He'd asked her a question. She reached a handful of snow and rubbed it into his face until he choked to a stop.

When he looked up at her with the crystals melting on his thick eyelashes, she melted as well. He and she, melting together, mingling strengths, shoring up weaknesses, filling cracks and pouring endless love back and forth.

The two of them, triumphant. Victorious together. Forever.

"Yes, Vicar John Barton, I will marry you." She forestalled his kiss with one finger in the air. "I'd like to add an addendum about those six or seven daughters. Would you consider mixing in a few sons?" She smiled down at him as she stroked the snowmelt from his cheek. "Handsome, kindly sons?"

He didn't reply. He simply wrapped one icy hand around the back of her neck and pulled her head down. Her heart pounding, she allowed it.

His mouth was firm and hot and heavens, he tasted as good as he smelled! The kiss went on and she began to learn, and then he began to moan and Norah breathlessly thought perhaps there was something to be said about this marriage idea, for the kiss was giving her all sorts of interesting notions.

She was surprised they didn't melt the snow to a river beneath them.

This man. I choose this one, above all others.

The miracle, the magic, the *blessing* of it all was that the man she'd chosen had chosen her right back!

He was warmth and strength and goodness and she thought that perhaps—just perhaps!—she truly did have a lovely smile, for she felt as if her entire being was smiling, body and soul.

The snow continued to fall upon them, as soft and light as a kiss.

Epilogue

A NOTHER YEAR, ANOTHER Christmas in Haven. Another pair of blessed lovers—or two!

The snow would fall until spring melted it into sweet water. The woods would turn green again—green and brown, mysterious yet welcoming, just like the kindly eyes of the vicar's new wife. The river would flow fast and the apple trees would bloom and then drop their blossoms to line the lane with drifts of pink and white, almost like snow.

Farewell, dear reader, until winter returns to Haven, and the true snow falls and Christmastide rises nigh.

And the next desolate heart calls out for love.

All Books by Celeste Bradley

Debut Novel

Fallen

The Liar's Club

The Pretender
The Impostor
The Spy
The Charmer
The Rogue
Wedding Knight
(a Liar's Club novella)

The Royal Four

To Wed A Scandalous Spy
Surrender To A Wicked Spy
One Night With A Spy
Seducing The Spy

The Heiress Brides

Desperately Seeking A Duke
The Duke Next Door
Duke Most Wanted

The Runaway Brides

Devil In My Bed
Rogue In My Arms
Scoundrel In My Dreams

༄

For more information about Celeste's books,
visit: CelesteBradley.com

For updates on upcoming books and events
by Celeste Bradley, you can join
The Voice of Society newsletter
and be the first in the know!

Reviews

Sleepless in Staffordshire (*Haven Holiday Book 1*)

"Celeste Bradley has written an achingly beautiful winter tale."
— C Lewis, Amazon Reviewer

"I love her characters I get so attached! I have everything she's written and they just keep getting better." — S Hill, Amazon Reviewer

"Yes, it's got funny parts, and yes it's light-hearted, but Bradley hits you in the feels right out of the gate and doesn't let go until the end." — Julie P, Amazon Reviewer

"This is classic Celeste Bradley at her best. It was both heart wrenching and heartwarming." — S O'Byrne, Amazon Reviewer

On Bended Knee (*Wicked Worthingtons Book 6*)

"... the conclusion was so satisfying on many levels... I highly recommend it to all romance fans, but especially those loving a wounded hero who finds healing." —rosesareblue.net

"I love this book because the characters dance off the page. ... The characters work so well, of course, because the author so clearly is in love with them, making writing about them a labor of love."
— Fastidious Kingdoms

"My favorite Worthington story yet! I know the difficult journey it is to love a veteran who returned home different than he left. I love that she fought her own war and that they saved each other. ... Ms. Bradley balances this truth and the hope that love can conquer all so beautifully." — Tal, Amazon.com reviewer

Wedded Bliss *(Wicked Worthingtons Book 5)*

"A little bit of everything—humor, secrets, betrayals, misunderstandings, sexual tension, breathtaking romance—adds up to a completely delightful read." — Kirkus Reviews (★ starred review)

"This installment is packed with hilarious hijinks, excellent twists, and a sparkling tension between Bliss and Morgan." — Publishers Weekly (★ starred review)

"WEDDED BLISS is brilliant! It sparkles just like champagne!" — Romance Junkies

I Thee Wed *(Wicked Worthingtons Book 4)*

"This book was so much fun, I want to eat it." — Smart Bitches, Trashy Books

"This hugely fun novel is charming and delightful the whole way through." — Publishers Weekly (★ starred review)

"I Thee Wed has all the charming vivacity, scintillating wit, and incendiary sensuality of the previous books in Bradley's incomparable, Regency-set Wicked Worthington series, making it a don't miss for anyone who cherishes superbly written historical romances." — Booklist (★ starred review)

And Then Comes Marriage *(Wicked Worthingtons Book 2)*

"The book is a signature Celeste Bradley novel with her wit and engaging writing style. Her characters and settings come to life on the page." —Night Owl Reviews (top pick)

"In her typical mad-literary-genius fashion, Bradley cleverly concocts ... one of the most wonderfully original and wildly entertaining romances of the year." —Booklist

About the Author

Photo © Charles M. Fitch 2014

CELESTE BRADLEY is the *New York Times* bestselling author of more than 24 Regency historical romances, including the extremely popular *Liar's Club* spy series and the *Wicked Worthingtons*. She has twice been nominated for the RITA Award by the Romance Writers of America. Before becoming a writer in 1999, Celeste was an artist who specialized in pottery and ceramic sculpture. Although originally from the South, Celeste now resides in New Mexico. "It is one of the last habitats of the Free Range Human." She is fond of food that someone else cooks, animals of all sorts, painting, drawing, reading, and grandbabies.

Made in the USA
Monee, IL
10 January 2022

88592210R00094